GUILTY VERDICT

Rosalie Battye

Battye
Burton-in-Lonsdale

First published February 1988
ISBN No 1 871022 01 0

©

Published by –
K. & R. Battye
3 Wood View
Burton-in-Lonsdale
Carnforth
Lancs LA6 3JT

Printed by –
R. D. Stansfield
Halifax
West Yorkshire
HX3 5AX

Chapter 1

It was a night of thick fog, not particularly chilly for the time of the year, but definitely unpleasant. It was as if a wet, white sheet had been thrown over the town, dulling sounds and obliterating vision. Even near at hand objects were phantomlike, sometimes there and sometimes not. For a brief second, fog lights of passing vehicles pierced the gloom, and dim shapes passed by with only a muffled swish of tyres on the wet road. This continual, unfamiliar sound in place of the normal roar of traffic, voices and industry, combined with the impression of white nothingness all around, gave the surroundings a strange, unearthly aspect. There was a sense of floating in a half-real world. But there was nothing unreal about the smoggy atmosphere, for the damp air was holding down the chimney smoke and petrol fumes. In short, it was the kind of evening no-one would choose to be out of doors. The town workers had long since departed for their respective homes and the remaining passers-by hurried on their various errands with curiously subdued feet and one thought in mind, to get indoors and shut out the depressing gloom of the streets as quickly as possible.

Only one person in the vicinity of the river bridge was in no apparent hurry. Seemingly undepressed by the weather, he stood there as if waiting for something and gazing, rather, with approval at the swirling fingers of grey murkiness around him. His breath hung in front of his face, and his hair and eyebrows were damp with globules of moisture. He was quite ordinary in appearance, the kind of man who might live down any respectable street in town. Nothing about him demanded a second glance, from his typically English face down to his conventional black shoes. Consequently, no-one seemed to notice him as he stood in a shop doorway. Even if others had not been too much intent upon their own affairs, it would doubtless have been all the same.

Faint strains of music came from one of the basements nearby. The man glanced upwards towards the Town Hall clock and smiled at himself when his gaze found nothing but flat whiteness. Consulting his watch instead, he decided it was time to move on. If he did not hurry, he should time it just right. Mother and daughter usually set off around seven o'clock. It was just to be hoped that the weather was not going to deter them, this particular Wednesday evening. Time would tell. He would play it by ear, postponing his mission until the following week if necessary.

He knew where he was going and he headed directly for his objective, the residential area to the west of the town. He walked along several streets, the lights from the windows of the town's biggest stores piercing the gloom and showing up the pavements. Then, leaving the shops behind, he found the lights had largely disappeared except for the dimmed street lighting, and he had to watch his steps more carefully. He directed his path towards the railway bridge, passing underneath at the precise moment a long, accelerating diesel left the station and rattled over above, intoning eerily its two note interval. A street of offices and official buildings came next, then the road joined the river, following its course for a hundred yards or so until the park swallowed up its lethargic waters under an umbrella of leafy branches. Not that the man could see a glimmer of the water tonight. He just knew that it was there in the blank nothingness to his left. The low stone wall between the man and the river continued to circumvent the park further on, interrupted only for the wrought iron gated entrance. He followed its topstones dimly outlined by the now only occasional street light and sometimes trailed his hand along its rough edges. His steps were silent, for he walked on a soggy carpet of autumn leaves, recently fallen from the branches above.

He was still feeling cheerful, although he was also beginning to feel the usual thrill of apprehension that always attended these excursions. Taking a deep breath, he deliberately put a reign on his nervous system, for he needed his wits about him, even at this early stage of the proceedings.

Turning an especially dark bend, he almost collided with a hunched-up, elderly gentleman hurrying, as much as conditions would allow, in the opposite direction.

"Pardon me. My fault," the younger man apologised pleasantly, a light, steadying hand under the other's elbow. Then, without waiting for a reply, he continued on his way.

It took only a few minutes more to reach the children's recreation ground and the same again to the beginning of the reputedly elite, residential area, a wide belt of detached houses sitting smugly at the edge of both town and country. These houses had once been the property of the so-called upper class and professional people, but it was obvious that times had changed in the last half century. True, business men and would-be important people were still to be found there in considerable numbers, but at the same time the fact remained that much of its glory had departed. The houses had become too big and too uneconomical in upkeep for present day families and therefore many had been split into two or three or even as many as four flats. Several of the gardens had been reduced in size by recent developments.

The man slackened his pace, carefully avoiding the lighter parts of the street. There was still a dampness in the air, but the mist was not as thick as it had been in the centre of the town, a fact which he noticed with a twinge of regret. But no matter. He was well practiced in what he described as his art, and professionalism in that art was second nature to him. He could not afford a moment's carelessness, for it had been the undoing of several of his acquaintances. An incidental thing like fog could definitely be used, but it was his professionalism he relied upon at such times.

It was in front of one of the largest houses that he stopped, looking around him carefully but without the slightest trace of furtiveness. All was quiet and still. Even the road was deserted of people and vehicles. Sodden branches hung over the garden walls, waiting for the slightest touch to shed their burden of water, but there was not even a breath of wind to oblige. It seemed as if the solitary figure on the road was the only thing to move as it casually but silently with gloved hand lifted the latch of the gate ostentatiously announcing 'Broad Acres'. This house and garden was quite obviously in its original form, though now somewhat neglected, seemingly unmoved by all the changes round about it. Because of the dull atmosphere the actual house was not visible from the road tonight, but the man knew that it normally presented an imposing face to the outside world, being positioned in the one gap between its screening bushes and trees. The

5

grounds were generous in size and park-like in character. The drive itself soon disappeared out of sight of the road, for it curved at an early stage behind concealing laurels. It was therefore unlikely that any watcher would have witnessed the sudden dash made by Broad Acres' unexpected visitor from the public highway to the impenetrable shadows in that private garden. Twenty yards from the house he stopped, invisible under the bushes. Water dropped on to his head and down his neck but the man scarcely noticed. His whole attention was focussed upon the house, now clearly visible, and upon the security of his own position. Satisfied as to the latter, he settled quietly to await movements from the house. Any further plans were dependent upon what transpired during the next ten minutes or so. It should happen within that time if mother and daughter were going to the usual Wednesday evening prayer meeting at the Oak Lane Church they attended, for the session began at seven thirty.

He had a reasonably good, if distant, view of the front of the house. There were lights behind two downstairs windows and one upstairs. The curtains were not drawn in one of the downstairs rooms, and the watcher slipped quietly across the lawn to another patch of darkness in a shrubbery which was nearer and in direct line with the room. His position was a little more vulnerable there but, even so, anyone would have had to stare very hard to see him, especially if he had come from the bright interior of the house. Certainly, as a viewpoint, his position was perfect. There was the front door a short distance away and the window he was interested in was the second to the left of the door. He could clearly see inside the slight, round-shouldered figure of Sir John Bentley Hampshire apparently watching television in the window corner of the room. There was no-one else in the room and every now and then Sir John's head kept falling forward as if he were nodding off.

The watcher frowned. Mrs. Hampshire and Katherine were going to be late if they did not go soon. Perhaps they were not going, after all, or had already gone before he had arrived. He needed to know, before he did anything. Scarcely had the thoughts crossed his mind when a female figure came into the scene before him, only for a moment, just long enough to plant a swift kiss on the distinguished brow of the elderly man and then she was gone again, leaving her husband almost immediately to resume his peaceful nodding. Then the upstairs light went out and another appeared in its place behind the glass of the front door. Mrs. Hampshire came out and closed the door behind her. The hidden man noticed with interest that she did not lock it. But where was the daughter, Katherine? Perhaps she was following, for the light was still on. Even as he pondered, a car engine purred into life in the distance and a rather old-fashioned model of a large saloon came round from the back of the house, pulling up for the waiting figure at the front entrance. A moment later they had gone.

The watcher of all these proceedings reflected that his calculations regarding the probable course of events at the Hampshire home had been remarkably accurate. He had made his plans accordingly, and he only hoped that his luck would hold out for the next half hour.

After about five minutes, with a last glance at the now clearly sleeping form of Sir John, the figure outside moved on silent feet towards the front door. A gentle touch with gloved hands at the handle told him that he had been right in his impression that it had been left unlocked and, swinging the door slowly open just enough for him to pass through, he found himself in a long, narrow hallway. The aristrocratic owner was in a room somewhere to the left, which was all to the good, for the unannounced visitor knew that the room he wanted was to the right. He hoped his informer was sure of his facts. His information had been useful but he was too naive to be used again, he reflected as he brought to mind his clear mental image of the layout of the Hampshire home. On noiseless feet he took the corner of the passage which led to the right hand part of the house. He counted the doors. One. Two. Three. This should be the one. He stood at the door and listened. Putting his hand to the knob, he opened the door, but only a fraction when he realized that a light was burning in the room. It was no doubt the other illuminated downstairs room he had seen from the outside. All his cautious instincts automatically took control of his actions. He stood there and listened again. Nothing but silence, except for the distant strains of television music and voices. His mind told him that no-one could be in the room. Only three people lived in the house, and he could account for all three of them. The housekeeper only came in during the day. Imperceptibly, without rushing, he pushed at the door, half an inch at a time, until he could see into the room. It was empty as he expected. He found himself looking into Sir John's library, where books lined every wall. Apart from books, the room was sparsely furnished, containing only a desk, a chair and a cupboard, items small in quantity but of high quality. The only other large object in the room was the thing which caught and held his attention, a metal safe. He closed the door behind him, his chest thumping in anticipation, and walked across the room. He could hide behind the floor-length curtains if anyone came. Kneeling in front of the safe, he set to work. Safes were his business, and this one was unlikely to beat him. He worked carefully and patiently, his ears ever alert for approaching footsteps. In a matter of only several minutes, he was straightening up again, the Hampshire diamonds safely in his pocket.

Having got what he came for, he had no desire to linger, but he did not lose his cool carefulness. Ever alert, he returned the way he had come and reached the outside door without mishap. Someone was talking in a very low voice on the television, just the necessary monotone background to keep the old man asleep. The visitor had thick, soft soles to his shoes, but he didn't need them here for the carpets were thick and cushioning. The outer door opened silently at his soft touch and he went back out into the night, closing it slowly after him. But not slowly enough. Suddenly, nearly startling him out of his skin, a piercing screech cut the grave-like silence. The man froze in his tracks, automatically relaxing his hold on the door handle. The cat, which was taking the opportunity afforded by the open door to get inside its own home, glared up at him, swishing its tail, probably more in fright than in pain, and disappeared inside and along the hall at an incredible speed. The man had obviously unwittingly trapped some part of its anatomy in the door. His alarm changed quickly to annoyance and unaccustomed panic. This was the nearest his visits had ever been to setting off a burglar alarm! He could truthfully say that he had previously never found himself in as tight a corner as this could be likely to prove. The noise had been enough to rouse the whole neighbourhood. It was incredible that one small animal could have produced such a blood-curdling scream! He must get away before prying eyes came to investigate. He slipped into the bushes from whence he had watched the window earlier. Two things happened almost immediately. The door opened to silhouette Sir John Bentley Hampshire peering out into the darkness and, apparently from a side gate, a tall man with rolled-up shirt sleeves was approaching the dark shrubbery at a run on his way to join the other man. The intruder sank deeper into the bushes, heedless of the uncomfortably wet conditions, for the light from the house came perilously near to reaching him.

"Is everything alright, Sir John? We thought we heard . . . "

"Exactly. Something made a row." replied the man in the doorway. "But all seems to be quiet now, Donald. Nobody here getting murdered. Come inside, do. Such a night."

"All right, if only to help you make sure you haven't a burglar inside." the other replied, then laughed, "though they would hardly announce their presence with a noise like that!"

The figure in the bushes moved rapidly once the two men had gone indoors. Crossing the lawn, he went from one darkly shadowed area to another with many glances at the house where the door had been left open and the light blazing. He paused, with each glance, until he was sure it was safe to go on. The last time he looked that way, he froze to the spot again, for once more there was someone looking out. At that distance, and with the mist beginning to swirl around again, he could not be sure which of the two men it was. Had they seen him? He decided that his appearance would be as indistinct to the man in the doorway as the man's was to him. Then there were two of them again. He could not tell what they were saying. A grey figure moved across the garden the way it had come, from the side, apparently running. The hidden man thought he must risk running, too. Edging to the back of a tree trunk, he ran towards the road, making sure to keep the tree between himself and the door of the house. He paused only once. Satisfied that there was no longer anything to cause him alarm, he continued in a more casual fashion to the garden gate and so, gaining the security of the street, he gave a sigh of relief.

There was no-one in sight, but he deliberately turned right at the gate instead of the way he had come. He reflected that this perfectly good alternative route held the most cover and that it would probably sooner enable him to mingle with other people. Proceeding at normal walking pace, and still assuming a nonchalant air, he made for the town again, his tense nerves relaxing a little more with every step. For a brief, alarming period he had foreseen calamity, that the loss of the diamonds had been discovered and that he would be caught. Surely there had not been time for the jewels to be missed. Such a discovery would have been too close for his own safety. But he was alright now, however close to detection he had been for a time. Though the diamonds felt to be burning a hole in his pocket, he knew that anyone suspicious would have to have X-ray eyes to suspect they were there. There was no flaw in the impression he gave of respectable citizen intent upon his own affairs. Under an avenue of trees he exchanged nods with a passer-by, who did not give him a second glance. Now completely at ease, he hurried on.

He was halfway back to town before he began to suspect that he was being followed. He was not sure and he told himself that it was just his acutely trained perception that was anticipating the possibility. It was not so much that he could hear footsteps as that every so often he heard what could only be described as the suggestion of a sound, a swish, a rustle, just some simple movement that jarred his senses. It became more difficult to be sure of anything one way or the other as traffic and people increased on the street, and the mist which had been good to him on his night's mission now was acting against him. If he was being followed, his pursuer would be able to keep close. He had to know, somehow, if anyone was there. His mind ran on more quickly than his feet, considering the road ahead and seeking some means of temporarily discarding the diamonds into a safe place as a precaution and without attracting attention to himself.

He had come to an area of terraced houses, blocks of flats and small council gardens. He paused in an archway and waited to see if anyone overtook him, in particular, the shirt-sleeved man Sir John had addressed as Donald. While he stood there, a police car cruised past, its headlamps piercing the vaporous gloom.

He was puzzled and wished he knew what had happened at Broad Acres since he left. Could the police be on their way there? Surely not, but the sooner he got rid of the incriminating evidence the better. He did not care for this uncertain feeling.

No-one the man considered to be significant passed his archway, so he set off again, impatient not only to dispose of the diamonds but also to get into some dry clothes, for he was very wet. Nevertheless, he was glad he had not used a car on the job. They could be too incriminating — better avoided on local jobs. People were apt to notice a strange car sitting waiting in an urban district. He was glad also that he had undertaken this exercise himself, being conceited enough to consider that one of the others would have been more likely to bungle the whole thing in panic. No, providing there was no mishap in the next few minutes, everything had once again gone reasonably according to plan, with the usual successful results. It was the cat which had brought him so near to disaster. How ironic it would have been for him, with all his experience, to have been betrayed by a mere animal! He told himself now, a reasonable distance away, that there had not really been any danger of that.

In spite of his hearing nothing and seeing no-one while hiding in the archway, the intangible sounds returned as soon as he stepped out again. Turning round suddenly, he momentarily saw a light shape dodge into the shadows and he became worried again. He hurried past a long row of large houses with Edwardian frontages and white railings and rounded the corner. For just a few moments, until the other man also reached the bend in the road, he was out of his sight.

Suddenly, he acted upon impulse, a thing he seldom did. Right to the edge of the pavement where he stood was a more commonplace building than the stately row he had just passed, a building he knew to be a block of four flats. Moreover, he knew that one of them belonged to young Christopher Meyer, son of Pastor Meyer of the Oak Lane church attended by the Hampshire ladies. In the light of several pressing invitations, it was time that he paid him a social call. He knew from the drone of music that he was at home, for his were the first windows overlooking the road. Without hesitation he went into the common vestibule. There, knocking lightly at the door of Number One, he went straight inside Christopher's flat. He found himself in what was obviously his kitchen. The boy had been making coffee, for the jar was still beside the kettle, sugar and wet spoon nearby and a strong aroma in the air. From the sounds of animated conversation beyond the closed sitting room door, Christopher obviously already had a visitor. The knock on the door must not have been heard, for the conversation continued. The newcomer stood looking irresolutely round. Christopher was comfortable enough here. Gossip had it that the manse had been too straight-laced for him — until recently, that was, when he himself had professed some kind of religious experience. Curious, the drawing powers of religion! It would be intriguing to question him sometime.

The visitor idly reached out to push in a drawer left partly open, but it refused to move. It was a towel drawer and without feeling any sense of taking liberties he removed the drawer and then the towel which had fallen down the back. On point of replacing the drawer he stopped and, with a quick movement, slipped a hand in his pocket and placed the diamonds behind the drawer. It would be easy enough to retrieve them from there at his leisure. The drawer fitted in front of them alright. He straightened up. Still the voices droned on. With a slight bow towards the closed door hiding the speakers, he went back into the damp and the fog.

Chapter 2

Once again justice was satisfied. The law had been applied and the accused tried, judged and found guilty. It was happening every day all over the country and retribution being meted out to suit the crime. Juries met and considered evidence, the impartial custodians of men's fortunes, whether the case be simple in nature or complex. Certainly the jury had been in little doubt as to the direction of the evidence in the case of the Hampshire diamonds. It all pointed to the guilt of the accused. True, there were certain things left unexplained, such as the loud noise which had triggered off the investigations, but it was agreed that no explanation could in any way alter the evidence against him. It had not been considered to be of any relevance that he was the son of a minister, for it was not always 'like father, like son'. It had counted more that about twelve months ago, left alone to face the music after some prank with a not too scrupulous gang of youths he had for a short while associated with, he had had a strong warning addressed him by the voice of the law.

During the trial, the papers were full of the case and, glad as usual to find the moral life of a minister's household brought down to its own level, fallible and imperfect, the public enjoyed the brief scandal.

'Diamonds become the pearl of greatest price to minister's son', the headlines stated in one account. Beneath this distasteful witticism, the story of the case was told in full, with pictures of Christopher to give colour to the narrative. It was quite a long article, and extracts will suffice here.

'Christopher John Meyer, the son of Pastor Martin Meyer, minister of Oak Lane Church, was yesterday sentenced to five years' imprisonment for the theft of the Hampshire diamonds. The valuable heirloom is in the form of necklace and bracelet, and their disappearance was from the outset of the affair suspected to be only the latest incident in a series of national thefts of art goods and jewellery. It is thought that Meyer, the accused, was but 'used' by the master mind of a larger organisation, knowledge of which has so far baffled the authorities. Meyer could not, or would not, divulge any information which might be helpful towards any future arrests. On the contrary, Meyer constantly affirmed his ignorance of any such organisation and his innocence of this particular crime. However, no statement of his evidence could be corroborated but was rather very much loaded against him, so much so that the jury returned a unanimous verdict . . . '

' . . . Witness, Mr. Donald Guest, from the house next to Broad Acres, the Hampshire residence, gave a graphic account of the evening's events. Just after seven thirty, he had been seeing off a friend, Mr. Graham Lee (who also verified his account), from his own doorstep when what sounded like a scream came from the direction of Broad Acres. Asking Mr. Lee to wait until he returned, Donald Guest had rushed to his neighbour's house where he found the owner, Sir John Bentley Hampshire, also investigating the noise at his own door. Nothing seemed to be amiss. A quick inspection of the rooms revealed no-one in the house and Mr. Guest had gone back to the door to investigate outside before returning to his friend. Immediately, he had caught sight of a movement in the Broad Acres garden. Rapidly returning to Mr. Lee, he had instructed him to join Sir John, with an injunction to check that nothing was missing from the house, and not pausing to don shoes or coat, he had sprinted to his own gate, just in time to hear the click of the next garden gate and to see a dark figure pass his. As there was no-one on the road at the other side of Broad Acres, he was sure that the person was the one he had seen in the garden. There was no car in sight and the man started to walk away. He had followed the other at a discreet distance and with much difficulty due to the fog to the area where the accused now lived. Turning the corner by the flats, he found that his quarry had disappeared, a fact suggesting that he had turned in there. Mr. Guest had then, after a moment or two's consideration, departed in search of a telephone box where he had made his report to the Police Station. By that time, moreover, the theft of the diamonds had been reported and a man sent out on the job. However, his presence was requested at the station to make an official report . . . Asked in court whether he was certain the person he had followed was the accused, he admitted that he could not swear to it because of the fog, but that the general height and build were the same . . . '

'Sir John in his statement said that Meyer had already been at his house that evening and had seen the diamonds in the room from which they were later stolen. More than that, he had actually delivered the bracelet from Raynor's jewellers where he, Christopher, worked. A minor alteration had been made to the clasp and its return had been promised for that evening. Mr. Raynor, feeling ill when the time came, had asked Meyer, one of his most trusted staff, to take it when he left the shop. Sir John had asked him in and, foolishly perhaps, but as a matter of interest and pride, had shown him the famous diamond twosome. He was extremely sorry at the turn of events for he had liked the young man in question. He struck him as of an open, direct character and on the said visit there had been nothing strained or unnatural about him. Yet he could do nothing but report the incident . . . '

'Throughout the whole case, Meyer insisted that he had no idea how the diamonds had got behind the drawer in his flat, nevertheless admitting his earlier contact with them. After leaving Sir John's house, he had not given the diamonds another thought until the police had arrived to search . . . However, he could not satisfactorily account for his actions on the evening in question, as not one of his statements could be verified. According to him, he had gone back to town after delivering the bracelet to have fish and chips instead of making his own evening meal, and on the South Bridge he had met a man depressed and intent upon drowning himself. Having managed to dissuade him, he took him back to his flat around seven o'clock where they talked until after quarter past eight, when the man had left in a much improved state of mind. He had promised to look Christopher up again sometime if that improvement was maintained. The police had not been able to trace the man as Meyer could only say that his name was Tony. He did not know where he lived. The police, he said, had only missed him by five minutes when they came to his flat. Unfortunately, during that five minutes Meyer had already eliminated all signs of his having had a visitor by washing up and clearing away the coffee things, the only slight shred of evidence that might have given credence to his story. No-one in the other flats could or would testify to his having any visitor that night. In addition, in the summing up, it was pointed out that Meyer knew exactly where the diamonds were kept at Broad Acres, that it was difficult to imagine any motive for a third party to have put them in his flat, and that the thief was on foot and Christopher had no car . . . Meyer remained calm and self controlled, even when the verdict was given against him. Paster Meyer said afterwards that it had not taken them by surprise and that the jury could not be blamed in the light of the evidence. He himself believed that the truth must lie in a different direction and he could only hope that before long that truth would come to light and Christopher's position be vindicated.' There, the newspaper account ended.

On the whole, public opinion joined with the official in that there was no chance of miscarriage of justice, that Meyer must be a liar as well as a thief, albeit a thief in someone else's pay. Consequently, he could not complain that he would lose his freedom for five years as he served the time of his prison sentence, or that he had lost his job and his reputation for always.

Even the hardest criminal has his supporters, be it merely mother, wife or child. With Christopher Meyer, professing to be no criminal at all, the loyal band of supporters was not so limited. His defendents loudly proclaimed his innocence but could not prove it. Among these were his family, his friends and many of his fellow members at his father's church. Even during the trial concerted prayer went up from the church that he might be exonerated from blame. When the verdict of 'guilty' was given there was still confidence in a wise Providence who was in control not only of His own universe but also of the affairs of men, even when they could not understand His sovereign ways. Maybe there were a few who did not know Christopher so well who in their hearts were not so sure. After all, if he were not guilty, surely his condemnation would not have been allowed to happen. Even those who believed in him admitted sometimes that they were tempted to ask 'why'?

Pastor Meyer and his wife, after the ordeal was over, had been advised to go away for a break, however brief, but they worked harder than ever instead. They determined not to shirk their responsibilities because of their own personal troubles, but rather chose to be examples in demonstrating the victory and comfort to be had in the God they served. Besides, there was a certain amount of consolation to be had from work and working. The pastor's face bore little trace of the inner turmoil and his messages were of increased intensity. The only evidence of stress in Christopher's mother was in her unaccustomed quietness. The younger brother and sister of Christopher, with their lack of experience, were taking longer to come to terms with the unexpected crisis, especially Elizabeth, volatile and honest as she was. To them all this was not just 'a case', a source of excitement or interest in its duration then over for good. It was something they had to live with day after day, month after month and year after year.

24

Chapter 3

Paul Ransom was neither awake nor asleep. He was hovering in that in between state, dimly conscious of his surroundings with their accompanying shapes and sounds, and yet his eyes refused to open again and the suggestion of dreams had begun to be mixed with reality. One reason why sleep did not overome him completely was that the evening was unseasonably close and he was hot, even though his bedroom window was open. Another was that he was trying too hard to sleep. His parents were away on a fortnight's late holiday and any minute now the motherly lady they had always referred to as Aunty Janet would come in from next door to tuck him up like a baby. He might be a disgusting number of years younger than his brother David but he *was* thirteen, and a teenager was too old to be tucked up. Therefore, if he were asleep, he would know nothing about it. Fondly, he realised that she was doing her best for them in their parents' absence and, truth to tell, apart from her gently guiding hand Paul would have been inclined to stay up until his brother's bedtime. This adopted aunt had firmly dispelled any such ideas. I wouldn't have been as bad, somehow, to have had David looking in at him for that would not have been fussy 'mothering'.

Before the desired oblivion came, Paul heard the unwelcome tread on the stairs. He resigned himself to the usual feigning of sleep. He was always afraid that one night she might even go to the extent of kissing him, the very height of affrontery. The ordeal was short and sweet, completely out of proportion with the great endurance test he had made the visit in his mind. Aunty Janet simply adjusted the covers here and there, murmuring a few soothing words to the apparently sleeping figure and departed, amusement on her face at the way of boys, leaving him more awake than ever.

He stared through the window into the darkness. Then he saw the winking light of an aeroplane passing from the wardrobe to the bathroom side of his window and he could hear its faint drone in the stillness. He had a good mind to put the light on and read for a while.

Before he had time to suit action to thought, he heard the outside door and then voices below. It was a female voice which sounded like that of Elizabeth Meyer, Christopher's sister, talking with his own brother, David. They had only seen Liz once or twice since her brother had been sentenced and that was at church when she and her other brother, Alan, had had very little to say. Both of these facts were unusual as the younger generations of both families normally spent most of their free time together, occasions when there was seldom any shortage of words!

Suddenly jolted into action by the sounds below, Paul threw back the bedcovers and crept out of the room to the top of the stairs. He had no desire to miss any of this conversation in case there was anything said to throw fresh light on the problem uppermost in all their minds. He was keeping a file on all the information he could gather concerning the Hampshire diamonds affair. Pathetically, it seemed one had to achieve a certain magical age before being taken seriously, therefore, he kept it hidden. Considering the time and mental energy devoted to studying those bewildering researches, he was confident he would eventually discover the truth and unmask the real culprit single-handed — or, more realistically no doubt, he might stumble on some new tenuous clue just worth passing on to someone more able to follow it up.

To go openly and join the two downstairs would only mean getting sent back to bed by David and result in their keeping an eye on the door, therefore it was best to eavesdrop. They had closed the living room door so that he would not be disturbed, so he crept down the stairs in the darkness and into the coat cupboard in the hall directly outside the room,

27

leaving the door ajar. There, he knew from past experience that he would be able to hear every word. He didn't approve of eavesdropping, but on several occasions he had deemed it to be both justifiable and necessary!

"I didn't really come to talk about your parents, however," Liz was saying as Paul made himself comfortable. The pause that followed was so long that he began to be mystified, then he heard the girl blurt out, "David, what are we going to do about Christopher?" Liz never bothered to beat about the bush.

David was obviously taken aback by the question for there was an equally long silence in which Paul could well imagine his brother's bewilderment.

"We?" David said eventually. "What *can* we do?"

"That's what I want to talk about. Mum and Dad and Alan have gone out but I stayed behind so that I could come and see you."

"But every detail has been investigated. The matter's finished. What's the use of even talking now? — Though we will by all means if you've had some new thoughts."

"I thought *you* might have if . . . You are regarded as something of an intellectual, David, and if Christopher is innocent there must be a flaw, a mistake or a clue somewhere in all this mess!"

"I'm not a detective! What can I do — send out an SOS for the right criminal and twist his arm until he confesses?"

"I'm not asking *you*, individually, to do any-

28

thing," the girl replied pleadingly. "I only want to . . . to discuss things to see if anything *could* be done, or found out. I don't want to talk to Mum and Dad about it. They've been through enough. And they find it easier to accept than I do. But I . . . I can't just sit down and take it all without being convinced everything possible has been done."

"But the evidence has already been considered," David repeated with emphasis, "and everyone satisfied that he is guilty. *You* don't think he is guilty and I don't think he is guilty, but how do we convince anybody else of that? They'd just say we were biased . . . "

"I don't *think*, I *know*!" Liz interrupted passionately and Paul could hear the break in her voice, but he knew that she would not cry in front of his brother however much she felt like it. In his cupboard, he wondered vaguely if he should be listening in to this conversation but he did not move.

"Stop parading about and sit down, to start with," David said next in a somewhat patronising, adult voice, "and we'll talk. But, honestly, I don't see what we can do besides talk." There was a pause. "You might not like it, but the question to begin with is what makes us so sure that Christopher is not guilty, after all? The evidence was pretty convincing and, if he is the thief, we are wasting our time even talking."

"I'll begin to think that you are not on his side, either!" Liz cried impatiently. "You know Christ-

29

opher as well as I do. Even in the days when he got up to pranks with those other lads when he went into the flat at first he would have absolutely drawn the line at something like this. He went because he felt 'restricted by religion', as he put it, not because he felt drawn to crime! And since he was . . . was converted, he is a hundred times less likely than ever to be involved."

"Church-goers do get into trouble."

"I'm not talking about his church-going. I'm talking about his *conversion*, which is a different thing entirely. Christians aren't people who just go to church, they are people who belong to Christ, as you should know after hearing Dad's sermons for so long," Liz retorted.

"It doesn't seem as if his conversion, as you call it, has done him much good," David replied sceptically. "Look what has happened to him almost immediately. You'll never convince me there is any advantage in becoming religious."

"We don't come to Christ for our temporal advantage, David," Liz protested wearily, "but for our sins to be forgiven and our lives put right."

I'm sorry, Liz." David was getting annoyed. "Sunday School stuff is intended for the age group it serves. Adults grow up in thinking as well as in stature. We live in an enlightened age. Our society has a scientific, intellectual mind. It seems incredibly naive to find any credence in that sort of religion any more . . ."

"Quote, page 100, paragraph 3, 'Twentieth

Century Religion'," Liz snapped sarcastically. "You mean it sounds naive to *you*, because you don't want to face the implications."

"I'm generalising, not talking of anyone in particular. But if you want to bring in names, Dr. Mason is a good example of what I mean. He is as gracious and generous a man as there could be, but he is also a realistic and thinking person, and I admire that."

Elizabeth snorted disdainfully. "You make me mad! I like Dr. Mason as a person, but that doesn't excuse him for his scepticism. Can't you see that it is arrogant to think you know better than God? Neither of you benefit much from Dad's sermons! But at least Dr. Mason discusses his views graciously! Thinking people! You regard yourself as a thinking person but all you do is trot out the usual trite observations. The human mind isn't greater than God. One day you'll find you're not quite so self-sufficient, after all. And I'm going, for you are not going to be any help!"

Once again, Paul could tell that Elizabeth was close to tears. Always of a tempestuous nature, her taut nerves were stretched almost to breaking point after her recent ordeal, and Paul marvelled that David could be so provocative and thoughtless in the circumstances, thinking person or not! As always, Paul's feelings rose to Liz's defence as she was one of the few people who treated him as an equal and not as a child.

David's apology was genuine this time. "Come

31

back," he urged contritely. "I'll listen. We'll talk. We . . . I've got off the subject. What have you got on your mind? Was it some particular thought that brought you here tonight?"

"Not really. Only I thought . . . that is, more or less what I've said, that if we could all meet together to talk and talk and talk, say at Christopher's flat where we could also have a thorough search, maybe we could . . . The police have been over it, so we probably wouldn't find anything, but we could at least all put our heads together to see if there is anything else . . . Four brains are better than one."

"I have an idea that you have more in your mind than you have admitted to," David replied. "Tomorrow night then. But I don't know about Paul," he added doubtfully.

"Oh, David, we must include Paul! He's probably quicker thinking than all of us."

David laughed. "That's what I'm afraid of," he said. "He's liable to come to some private, weird solution of his own and go tearing around putting his foot in it."

"Oh, surely not. Let him come."

"You don't know him as well as I do. He . . ."

Here, the agitated subject of their conversation, forgetting his cramped position, trod on a broom which catapulted the handle against the opposite wall of the cupboard. Paul knew that he was in trouble if he did not move — fast! Leaping quickly but carefully out of the cupboard, the unashamed eavesdropper turned towards the stairs and took them two at a time. On the landing, knowing that he was out of sight of the living room door, he slowed down and tiptoed to his bedroom.

"I tell you, I bet that was Paul," David was saying when the downstairs door opened. "Where are you, you young rascal?"

An abortive search could be heard down below as the hall and coat cupboard revealed nothing of any guilty eavesdropper.

The stairs light went on and there were sounds of footsteps approaching, two lots of footsteps. Liz was with David. She wanted to see for herself how Paul would get out of that one.

Paul's bedroom was suddenly filled with light and a very surprising sight met two pairs of eyes. There in bed, his arm stretched over the pillow, was David's younger brother, eyes closed and his face apparently flushed with sleep.

Liz did her best to subdue a chuckle. "I admit something made a noise but it wasn't him, that's certain!" she whispered and they went out, leaving him again in darkness.

"I wonder," Paul heard his brother mutter doubtfully. "We tell that lad he is just made to be an actor, but he says he wants to do something more 'useful to the community' like being a policeman or, better, a private detective! It is a wonder he has not already put up a door plaque advertising Sherlock Ransom!

Paul grinned to himself in the dark, satisfied.

Chapter 4

By teatime the next day, David still had not said anything to Paul about the plans for that evening. He didn't even get round to wondering why Liz had requested this meeting for the more pressing problem of whether to take Paul along with them. Debating the matter all day, his sense of caution was largely uppermost. Nevertheless, he could not help but feel pangs of disloyalty at the thought of leaving his brother out. Liz would no doubt take her younger brother, but David told himself that Alan was not as young as Paul, and far more sensible. Paul would be disappointed in them for, despite the difference in their ages, the four, together with Christoper, had kept pretty much together. David had no clear picture of what he feared might happen if they took Paul with them. He could not deny that his brother was, as Liz had implied, quick of perception. The trouble was that with all his teenage impetuosity he was liable to forget about discretion being the better part of valour. In the end, feeling responsible for Paul in his parents' absence, he kept his counsel and played for safety. Anyway, Paul seemed intent upon his own affairs and disappeared as soon as he had finished his tea.

David set off as soon as he could, but even so he was late. He had had a rush, for he had extra responsibilities in the home while they were on their own. He felt rather annoyed with his brother for vanishing so quickly, for he could have done with a bit of help, and was reasonably certain that Paul had not done any homework, either.

He reached the park gates a little later than their prearranged time and found Elizabeth and Alan waiting for him there.

Liz did not reproach him for that, but her look was disapproving, all the same. "I'm sorry you haven't brought Paul," she said accusingly.

David raised his eyebrows and shrugged his shoulders but did not reply.

The quickest route to the flat led through the park. Though it was a place they had spent many happy hours, the leafy avenues held no attraction for them tonight. They did not notice the branches rustling above them, the colourful fallen leaves beneath their feet, or the pleasant smells of autumn in their noses. For the most part they did not even talk to each other but walked with their hands in their pockets, their heads down, tired and dejected. David's whole demeanor spoke of resigned futility.

After all, it was a big thing they were up against. If there had been any flaw in the case the police would have spotted it. They were trained in these matters. There had not even been a finger print out of place. Alan was little different from his usual quiet self. Only Liz, despite her drooping posture, displayed any signs of animation. There was a silent determination about her, and David could not help but admire her for it.

"Sir John was at church again on Sunday morning," David observed. "He seems to have taken it all very decently."

Elizabeth nodded. "He's a member at the Abbey Church, really, as you know," she replied, "even though the ladies come to us. But he has come with them more than ever recently. Mum and Dad say that he has been marvellous with them, his whole attitude one of sympathy and regret, and Dad wonders if he doubts Christopher's guilt, deep down." She sighed and they lapsed into silence again, their thoughts following the line that David had started. The Meyers could well have been ostracised by Sir John, in the circumstances. After all, he had been the victim of the theft. It was his house Christopher was accused of entering. He was no longer young, and the events of that evening must have unnerved him somewhat. And yet he went out of his way to commiserate with the family of the one convicted! Liz reflected that that fact must have been a consolation to her parents.

The trio emerged from the park, crossed the road

and hurried along an alleyway which was a short cut to Christopher's old home. There was a nip in the air and they would be glad to get indoors. But when they opened the door, the flat felt only a little less chilly, and they did not feel welcome. There was something forlorn about the cold and silence. All the warmth had gone with its owner. It was clean and tidy, but did not feel lived in any more.

They went in and switched on a fire, glanced round the small kitchen and through it to the room beyond, then looked helplessly at each other. Now that they were here, they all felt to be wasting their time, not knowing what to do or say. Liz put the kettle on, primarily for something to do, and David paced about idly, frowning. Alan sat down and looked thoughtful.

"There is very little noise from the other flats," he commented. "It's not surprising Christopher's neighbours never knew he had a visitor that night."

They listened to the faint drone of music seemingly coming from the flat below. Apart from that, the only sound was a muffled tapping nearer at hand.

David ignored the noises. "What now?"

Liz wheeled round from the kettle and looked pleadingly at him. "Don't look so pessimistic, David. We might feel discouraged, but let's try to forget that, shall we? Let's get busy. At least it will be *doing* something. Come on — the night's going. I suggest we examine everything in the flat and report if we find anything unfamiliar, however insignificant it might seem. If Christopher didn't put those diamonds in this drawer," she said indicating the one beside her, "then someone else did, and that someone else might have left some trace of his being here. We . . . Whatever *is* that noise?"

The tapping sound had suddenly increased in volume, startling them all.

"Spooks?" Alan suggested, grinning at their nervousness. Fair haired and of middle teenage years, Alan looked attractive when he smiled.

The noise died away.

"Let's ignore it," pleaded Liz. "There'll be some simple explanation. We must get on."

Feeling somewhat uneasy they did so, though David first opened the window and put his head out into the night. There was no-one there, so he also inspected the vestibule, but could not hear the sound there at all. Rejoining the others, he unenthusiastically prowled around with them, simply for Liz's sake. Several times he checked on items he did not remember seeing before, but each one proved to belong there.

"If only he'd never left home!" groaned Liz.

"Did he have many visitors?" David asked.

"Not of late — apart from us," she replied. "He had job enough keeping coffee in the pot for us! He was always complaining that it was empty again. As you know, he was coming home a lot more often and even considering giving up this place altogether." She looked at David and smiled. "He was beginning to think the manse was a better place to be, after all, and that it was wrong to pay rent for the flat when he could live at home for less and give the difference to some needy cause."

David grunted but was prevented from replying by another interruption, a crescendo of tom-toms much louder than before. The three visibly jumped. David didn't like it. It made the flat feel eerie and himself vulnerable. They gazed around, puzzled.

"It sounded to come from the cylinder cupboard," Liz observed as the noise once more grew less.

"It couldn't be the water pipes, could it?" Alan suggested.

Suddenly, enlightenment seemed to cross David's face and he strode to the cupboard, reaching for the handle. "Stand back you two. You never know what might come out!" With one bold sweep David exposed the interior of the cupboard. "I thought so! Out with you!"

The wide-eyed, guileless face of Paul grinned out at them, the sight of which cheered them all unaccountably. Nevertheless, David's face remained stern.

"It took you some time," Paul complained. "I was getting rather uncomfortable."

"I've a good mind to make you more uncomfortable still by putting you over my knee," David threatened, offering no helping hand as his brother emerged. "It's a good job we have sound hearts. So you *were* listening last night."

Elizabeth put a restraining hand on David's arm. "Don't scold him," she said. "He's here now, so that's that. And I'm glad."

Paul bowed. "A chap has to look after his own interests," he told them. "It isn't a nice feeling being left out of things, but I forgive you," he added magnanimously. "Perhaps you were going to call me in when you'd got nowhere yourselves — don't answer that one! But now that you have come, I have to inform you that there is nothing to find."

"Thanks, Clever. We'll decide on that," his brother retorted.

After half an hour they had all come to the same conclusion.

"I told you," Paul said complacently, "though I don't know why you looked through all the flat. The kitchen was all that was necessary."

"And how do you make that out?" But David knew as soon as the question was out.

"Of course," Alan replied. "Any intruder could only have come into the kitchen for Christopher not to know he had been. Christopher was in there all the time with the man he met on the bridge," he added, pointing to the adjacent room.

"That's right," Liz agreed. "And the diamonds must have been planted while that man, Tony, was in the flat, for Christopher said he was here from seven o'clock to quarter past eight, only five minutes before the police arrived. It was half past seven when the thief was seen escaping from Sir John's grounds."

"And Christopher and Tony must have been too engrossed to hear him when he came in," Paul added. "Anyway, it proves what I said about only searching the kitchen."

David felt irritated with his young brother, but one look at his serious blue eyes changed his irritation to a vague admiration. "We can't afford to jump to conclusions," he replied. "And things get moved, you know."

Alan was still thinking about Christopher's visitor. "It's a bit strange that Tony didn't leave his name and address."

"That seems queer to me, too," David agreed. "If Christopher had been so much help to him, you would expect him to want to keep in touch, to promise to write or to make some definite arrangement to meet again. But no. He didn't even say where he lived — in the Shetlands, for all we know."

"Christopher told us the answer to that one," Liz reminded them. "He said Tony had promised to get in touch with him again if all went well with him, but that he refused to be any more trouble if things didn't work out. Maybe he was a decoy to keep Christopher out of the way."

"But they met accidentally at the river, not here. He couldn't have known Christopher was going for fish and chips!"

"If only the police had come five minutes earlier!" Alan sighed.

"It's amazing they got here as soon as they did,"

Liz replied. "Even taking Donald Guest's prompt action into account, they lost no time."

Alan spoke again in his usual thoughtful manner. "Are we assuming that whoever took the diamonds simply turned in here when he realised he was being followed?"

"That seems to be just about it," David agreed. "He had to elude his pursuer somehow and get rid of the incriminating evidence. Suddenly finding himself out of sight of the one who was following him, what better chance could the thief have had than to turn in here? And by the time he was ready to leave, Donald Guest had gone to find a phone box."

"But that's one thing that puzzles me," Liz objected. "Can you really imagine anyone in those circumstances just turning into the nearest convenient house? How did he know it was safe to go in? He might walk into someone as soon as he opened the door. I think it would be more risky than staying in the street."

"Definitely risky," David agreed, "without knowing what was inside. That hadn't struck me before."

"Without knowing what was inside," Liz repeated. "So do you see the implications? It's been bothering me because . . . " She broke off, embarrassed.

Paul jumped to his feet. "It was someone who knew Christopher!"

David shook his head, inclined to reject the idea immediately out of hand. The notion was incredible.

"Or knew *of* him in a more impersonal kind of way — just enough to have the excuse for calling on him," Liz amended miserably. Admitted openly at last, the suppressed thoughts of the previous weeks came out reluctantly, as if she were ashamed of them.

David's scepticism showed on his face. "What exactly are you suggesting? That Christopher was deliberately framed?" He took the argument to its logical conclusion, a conclusion David, by the tone of his voice, obviously did not believe.

There was a shocked silence. The flush on Elizabeth's face showed that it was no new thought to her as it was to the younger boys who, unlike David, seemed more inclined to consider the possibility seriously.

"What other reason could there be in deliberately planting incriminating evidence upon him?" Alan agreed reluctantly.

"Nobody would want to do that to Christopher!" Paul interrupted indignantly.

"Then why go to the trouble of leaving . . . ?"

"Are you really serious? I always thought Christopher was popular with everyone," David objected, following on from Paul's ejaculation.

"He was popular with *most* people," Liz replied with significant emphasis.

"I always envied him his cheerful, friendly ways," Alan acknowledged shyly. "People liked him better than they do an introvert like me."

They all felt very unhappy.

"My head's in a whirl," Paul complained, going to the tap for a drink of water. He carried his glass back to the settee. "Perhaps this will cool it down."

David ignored him. "Right," he said purposely. "Let's take the matter a little further. Can any of you" — looking pointedly at Liz — "think of any specific person who would deliberately harm Christopher? Is there anyone, anyone at all, you know with any reason for doing so? I'm at a complete loss to think of anyone!"

David noticed that Liz did not shake her head as emphatically as the others. He could almost feel her inner agitation.

"Liz?" he queried and she flushed but raised her head in a defiant attitude for what she knew she had to say. At the same time her reluctance was obvious.

"Oh dear," she groaned. "I don't like suspecting individual people of something so serious."

"Who was it that wanted to pursue the matter?" David reminded her. "To think of possibilities doesn't mean you are going to accuse anybody. But if there's a motive, we'll have to consider the person who has it. Christopher can only be freed by involving someone else, ultimately. Well?"

Liz still looked unhappy. Alan came sympathetically to her rescue. "I bet she is thinking of John Barrett." he said.

Liz's hands went to her cheeks and they all knew he had hit a nail most soundly on the head.

"John Barrett?" David repeated. "I don't think

I've heard of him."

"I'm glad I haven't the only suspicious mind," Liz smiled wryly at her brother. "John Barrett is a cousin of ours."

"And he would have a motive?"

"I think you could say so, though I wouldn't have thought it a sufficient one to go to such lengths. However, you can't tell with people."

"Let's hear about him."

"All right. I'll explain," Liz said resignedly. "Grandad Meyer is the only person in our family with a lot of money," she began. "He lives in a stately home of the real old type, which is far too big for him, and there is a lodge at the gates into which he is eventually going to 'retire' . . . "

"He is already past retiring age, really," Alan interrupted helpfully.

" . . . The large house he has for some reason willed to his eldest grandson," Liz went on, "at his twenty first birthday or when he gets married — providing he remains in favour, of course. Christopher is the eldest and, as you can imagine, this scandal rules him out. Aristocratic Grandad has no time for Christopher now. John Barrett is second in line and he had made it clear all along that he wanted the house himself. In many ways he is a snob like Grandad, conceited, avaricious and openly hostile to Christopher ever since the will was made. He will be twenty one early next year, only about a month after Christopher, and he has also just announced his engagement, so I imagine he will be house hunting. We have heard that he is already going about bragging that Grandad's house is his, now. As far as Christopher is concerned, he could have had the house anyway, for he didn't particularly want it."

Paul, listening with wide eyes and open mouth, did not realise he was spilling his glass of water until his attention was drawn to the dark patch on the mat.

"A would-be detective should be more careful," David scolded. "This is Christopher's flat you are messing up. And I'd like to know how you got in, in the first place. I've a good mind to report you for illegal entry."

"Oh, I have my ways," Paul replied evasively and, kneeling down to pick up the mat, he added, "Anyway, it's clean water."

His back was to the rest of them, so they did not see the button which he took up from just under the edge of the rug. Paul put it impulsively into his pocket, carried the rug to the sink, wrung it out and rubbed it down with a dry cloth, but his mind was all the time on the button. He even paid no further attention to the continued discussion on John Barrett. It was an unusual button, very flamboyant, round, with hub and spokes like a wheel, not one that he remembered seeing on Christopher or anyone else. In fact, he could not imagine Christopher's ever wearing it. It might be of no significance, but he would look through Christopher's clothes before he left.

"If it was John, he was taking a tremendous risk in calling while Christopher was at home," Liz was saying when Paul returned to the present conversation.

"I don't suppose Christopher kept him supplied with a key," David retorted. "We've already said that that applies to anyone. Without a key, I suppose it had to be done while he was there. Perhaps they hid somewhere — in the vestibule, for instance — until a convenient time occurred."

They all went silent again. Rather than clarifying matters, they seemed to be complicating them.

"And to complicate things still further, I can think of someone else with a motive," Liz ventured apologetically after a while.

David groaned.

"And this is a person you have all at least heard of from Christopher," Liz continued. "That is Lester Addison who works — worked — with Christopher at Raynor's jewellers. He was plainly jealous of him. You see, Mr. Raynor obviously liked and trusted Christopher particularly, considering him good at the job and good with the customers. Therefore he was training him for much better things eventually, partnership or something. The trouble, from Lester's point of view, was that he had been there much longer than Christopher, and therefore should be the privileged one. He was rotten to him."

"Why did Mr. Raynor keep him on?"

"Oh, he was too clever to let Mr. Raynor see his

nastiness and Christopher would not tell tales."

"And Lester thought he might step into the line of prospective partnership if he eliminated the competition?"

"He was wrong, but he might have thought so."

"Did he actually threaten to do that?"

"Christopher never said so," Liz admitted.

Alan put a hand to his head as in perplexity. "There are so many peculiarities," he sighed. "But it strikes me that there is something very inexperienced about a thief who attracts attention to himself at the scene of the crime by making a loud noise, then brazenly enters a flat where the risk of detection is so high. I don't get it. It doesn't sound right."

"If only," Liz groaned yet again, "If only we could find that man Tony. Once he corroborated the story, Christopher would be free. That's all we are bothered about, really. I don't mind forgetting the other details and leaving them to the police. You are welcome to playing the detective, Paul!"

"And how do we find a man called Tony?" David asked, one eyebrow cocked at the girl. " — at least, the one we want. We could probably find a thousand Tonys, all the wrong ones."

Alan's face was unusually animated. "I think I could be on to something. The best course of action is to seek this Tony."

"But we don't know a single thing about him except his christian name," his sister objected.

"Of course we do," Alan retorted. "We know he

48

was in trouble, tried to commit suicide and went back to Christopher's home to talk. We also know the time it all happened and the date. All we need to do is to compress the details and advertise for him."

"You might have something there," David conceded slowly, "though it would not be easy to word. Nor is the right Tony bound to see it. How would we know which newspaper to put it in?"

"Well, it is the best suggestion we have come up with yet. In fact, it is the only one, so I vote we go ahead," Liz said firmly. It will mean we are at least *doing* something." She paused and David wondered how many times she had said that. "We have nothing to lose."

"With no risk involved for us," added David. "I don't particularly want to end up in jail with Christopher! If we get our man and Christopher is freed, we can leave the rest to someone more capable and I, for one, will be thankful."

Paul's eyes gleamed and he fingered the button in his pocket. While the others were discussing the details of the advertisement to put in the newspaper, he slipped away casually into the bedroom and began to go through Christopher's clothes. Of course, the button did not have to belong to the thief — it could even be Tony's — but it *might*. Christopher, he knew, was meticulous in cleaning his flat, to the extent of many 'ideal housewife' taunts, which certainly meant that the button had not been there for long. But Christopher's clothes all turned out to be of a definitely conservative type, and Paul was glad to find no wheel-like buttons attached to them.

"What are you doing, Paul?" Liz called from the kitchen. "Do you want locking in? We are ready to go."

"If he could get in, he can get himself out," David replied unsympathetically.

"Just coming," Paul replied, hurriedly closing drawers and wardrobe doors. "Have you worked out the wording already?"

"Not altogether," the girl admitted. "We've just done a rough draft. It would be a good idea to let someone read it through and give us advice on choice of papers, and so on. I suppose we could ask Dad," she finished uncertainly.

"He might stop us," Alan agreed.

"What about Dr. Mason?" David suggested tentatively. "He's an author and goodness knows what else. He'd probably be the best to help us."

Dr. Mason had gone out of his way to be friendly with the young people and they sometimes visited him in his modern house up the hill from the manse where he had lived since moving into the area about two years ago. Liz might not care for his theology, but she had every esteem for his practical knowledge and intellectual know-how.

They were unanimous and prepared to leave.

"Well, had we missed anything?" Liz inquired of Paul as she turned the key in the lock.

Paul merely smiled, taking the question as the joke for which it was intended. He could not understand himself for not sharing his discovery of the button with the others. It was certainly not because they had tried to keep something from him. He was not one to hold a grudge. It rather amused him to be able to keep up with them. Perhaps it was because of his preference to do things in his own way. Unlike David, he did not mind the thoughts of a bit of a confrontation, and his sense of justice made him every bit as concerned to bring the wrong doer to his just deserts as to free Christopher. Whatever happened, he had a feeling that they had a long way to go yet, and so they could afford to leave no stone unturned.

Chapter 5

The Meyer household always began the day in a way which would be considered by many to be old fashioned. Breakfast was followed by a reading from the Bible and a time of prayer. These times had taken on a greater significance of late. Always remembered was the missing member of the family, but Elizabeth felt that she needed the prayer far more than Christopher did! Ever impetuous, she found it difficult to accept calmly what had happened and to maintain a simple trust in God, like the rest of the family. She felt full of questions, frustrations and impatience.

"What's up, Girl?" her father asked fondly, regarding her screwed-up expression. "Let's share it."

Elizabeth got up, walked to the window, then came back and sat down again.

"David was saying the other night that he can't

understand why God would allow this to happen to Christopher."

"And you couldn't tell him."

She smiled at him. "You can read me like a book," she said ruefully. "I admit that I ask 'why', if not in the same tone as David."

"We live in an evil world, spoilt by the devil, and christians aren't exempt from trouble or disease or the victimisation of wicked men. But he'll learn all the sooner how to cope with trouble, won't he? It has already made him a man overnight, so to speak. He has the right attitude towards it. He has learned to trust in a new way. When I saw him the other night he reminded me of the story of Joseph, sold by wicked brothers to foreigners, then wrongfully thrown into prison. That seemed a bit tough on a young man but, according to the Bible, and that's how it turned out in practice, God intended it for good ultimately and was in the whole ordeal with Joseph. Christopher was wondering what the 'good' would turn out to be in his case."

"Maybe David will be converted through it — though I don't see how — he seems further away than ever because of it. My trouble is that I can't *wait*. I want to know everything *now!*"

"Then you know what your lesson in it is! Remember, 'Tribulation worketh patience' — not automatically, but if we use it aright. Perhaps David *will* be converted if he sees his friends acting like christians ought to act."

53

Alan broke into the conversation for the first time. "I think he resents our being christians," he said. "It probably wasn't so bad for him until Christopher and Paul joined the ranks, but he probably feels outnumbered now and therefore on the defensive."

Elizabeth, her mind reverting to Christopher, was after all on the point of mentioning to her parents their idea of advertising for Tony, but her father suddenly changed the subject, reminding them of the time. So the moment passed and Liz and Alan departed for the school bus, their minds weighed down with problems and searching for answers.

They both went to the same school. Alan was just one of a large number making up the main body of the school but Liz was a more priviledged member of the upper sixth. As such, she was allowed to leave the school precincts at lunch time. Today, she met David coming out of his place of work with a box of sandwiches in his hand. They had arranged to eat together in the nearby gardens if they could find a warm enough corner. David worked in an accountant's office and he was always glad to get away from figures and out into the open air for his lunch break, so they often met like this, if Liz was not on some kind of school duty.

The route to the gardens took them past Raynor's jewellers. As they drew near, the glass door opened and a tall, red-haired youth came out, turned the way they were going and walked on ahead, keeping a very brisk pace.

Liz grabbed David's arm. She pointed. "David," she said in a low voice, "that is Lester Addison. No, you're looking the wrong way! Didn't you see him come out of the shop?— *that* one with the red hair."

"Bother!" he replied. "I wasn't taking any notice. The hair should be easy enough to recognise again, but I wish I'd seen his face. Come on, let's follow him a while. He might turn round so that I can see his features."

"I don't particularly want him to think I am following him around," Liz objected. "I'd hate him to get the wrong idea! He'd certainly recognise me, for he's seen me with Christopher often enough."

David smiled down at her. "He'd think it an honour to be followed by you."

David had never said anything quite so direct to her before and Liz went deep pink.

"But if he turns round," he continued, satisfied at the effect his words had produced on her, "you can turn round too and pretend to be looking in a shop window."

Liz glanced at him out of the corner of her eyes, but he was now like a straining bloodhound, eager to be after a scent. He hurried on with a hand at her elbow, and she almost had to run to keep up with him. There were plenty of people milling around, so they could easily mingle with them and keep quite close. There was no difficulty in keeping sight of that red hair! Lester Addison never slowed nor turned, but strode on with an obvious purpose in mind.

"Perhaps he is going home for his dinner," Liz giggled once.

"He can go where he likes if he'll only just let me see his face first!" David smiled back.

He was not going home, but it appeared that his purpose *was* to eat, for he eventually turned without hesitation into a cafe and was already sitting inside by the window when the two drew level.

"He is determined that you shall not see his face!" Liz laughed, gazing at the same back view they had had all along.

David grimaced then looked at the girl with apology on his face. "Do you mind waiting a few minutes?" he asked. "I'm going inside. Shouldn't take too long to look at a face, but I'd better have a glass of milk, or something, for the look of the thing."

Liz nodded agreeably enough. "I'll be looking in Etherington's window," she said, beginning to move away, "seeking inspiration for Christmas presents. Don't be long or I'll desert you."

David followed a tall, broad shouldered man through the cafe door and up to the counter. The man bought a couple of sandwiches then walked across to join Lester Addison at his small table by the window. Surreptitiously watching while the girl got his milk, David was surprised to see the man hand over a small envelope which the redhead immediately pushed hastily into his pocket.

"For services rendered," he heard the man say.

David took his milk, paid for it and selected the

next table to the two men. There were other diners at his table already, but his curiousity had been aroused and he wanted to be as near as possible to the object of his interest. Lester, not knowing David, had no reason to suspect that he was his only motive for coming into the cafe. In fact, Lester took no notice of anything or anyone else but his companion. He kept glancing at the older man as if about to say something, but the other had become a stranger concentrating on his sandwiches. David found himself studying the appearance of the other man instead of Lester, and felt confident that he could not forget him with his dark, bushy brows and moustache, his dark skin and small eyes. Lester couldn't have been a greater contrast. David remembered what he had come in for and he deliberately stared at the youth as he leisurely sipped his milk. Under his colourful thatch, Lester had the fair skin common to most people with red hair and his face was round and inclined to be quite fleshy, but its features could only be described as nondescript.

David was about to get up and go when Lester Addison spoke.

"If you want any further help . . . "

The other man merely shook his head and continued to eat.

"It was easy enough getting the infor . . "

The man looked up, red spots on his cheeks and scraped back his chair to cover any further words that Lester might say. "The boss don't want any more help," he snapped angrily but in low controlled tones, "and remember, you know nothing. If you forget that, you'll find yourself in trouble." With that, he got up and hurried out leaving half a sandwich still on the table.

David was intrigued. He was glad that he had not missed the exchange. He had missed the odd word but had no difficulty in following the gist of the conversation. He had heard just enough to make him wish it had gone on a little longer. Whatever it was all about, Lester Addison was at that moment feeling small and annoyed.

Liz was standing where she had promised to be. David made her jump by blowing down the back of her neck.

"Well!" he greeted her. "That was most interesting."

"So it should be," Liz retorted. "You've been long enough."

"Did you see the man who went into the cafe in front of me?

"Thick set man with dark moustache? I saw him," she continued as David nodded, "because he almost trod on my toes when he passed us, and I remember thinking an apology would have been in order. He passed me again about a minute ago looking as if someone had trodden on *his* toes!"

David nodded again and glanced at his watch. He exclaimed in surprise. It was time they were getting back, Liz to the High School and he to work.

"We haven't time to eat now," he said regretfully

58

"I'm sorry. Are you alright?"

"I'm alright," she laughed. "I've been stuffing myself on the quiet all the time I've been window gazing. You'll have to do the same as we walk along."

As they walked, David recounted what he had seen and heard. Conversation was difficult because of the busy pavements and it was not until they had to separate that his story was fully told, taking into account all Liz's interruptions and questions.

"Do you think the dark man is a crook?"

"Put it this way," David replied slowly, "There was something not quite open about him. He certainly didn't want Lester Addison to talk — that is, he seemed afraid of what the lad might say — but that doesn't necessarily make him a criminal."

"I think we might be on to something, David," Liz cried excitedly before they parted. "If Lester would get involved in any kind of shady business, he wouldn't stop at damaging Christopher for his own ends, would he?"

"Steady on! Don't jump to conclusions," was all David replied, then added, "I'll call for you tonight on my way to Dr. Mason's."

The rest of the day seemed interminable to both of them. School work and people's finances seemed relatively unimportant compared with their own preoccupations. But, as usual, evening finally came.

When the little party set off for Dr. Mason's house, no attempt was made this time to leave Paul behind. After the previous evening they were all in it, for better or worse. Perhaps David still had qualms but he realised that Paul was just as keen as they were to help Christopher. He also had to admit that Paul was no more a child than they were where logic was called for, and they might want plenty of that before they had finished! A little of Liz's intuition added to their more reasoned approach, and there was no telling what they might discover!

Dr. Mason had moved into a newly built house when he came into the district about two years ago. It stood half a mile up the hill behind the manse and he had named it Fair Haven. "Not that I think Baker Hill exactly fits the description," he had laughed wryly, "but it reminds me that I have several 'Fair Havens' in more sunny climes that I can visit whenever I get fed up with the fog and rain here!" He spent so much time away, whether on business or enjoying his 'sunny climes' that people did not think he was at home long enough to get fed up with anything!

Liz was hoping that he would be at home tonight as they climbed the hill. They should have checked. He had certainly been 'in residence' the previous weekend, for he had been in her father's congregation both Sunday morning and evening. He had spoken to her about some books he could send for Christopher to read.

"I wonder why Dr. Mason has never got married." she mused as they drew near.

"He has more sense," was Paul's quick, teasing

retort. "I feel no need of such an encumbrance, so why should he? I only hope I feel the same in ten years!"

"He probably thinks someone might marry him more for his money than for himself," Alan suggested. "I mean — he wouldn't be likely to find out until it was too late, would he?"

"He certainly copes alright without one — without a housekeeper either," Liz acknowledged. "He once told Mum jokingly that housework wasn't the big bogy women made out — he managed to do all his domestic chores while he was waiting for the toast to brown!" She sighed, "Domesticated as well as clever."

"While most of us are neither," laughed Alan.

"Speak for yourself," Paul rejoined.

"I keep telling you he is a clever man." David joined in the conversation for the first time. "Because you do not like his philosophy you seem to think you mustn't admit it. My boss would tell you what a respected man he is, with lots of influential contacts. He has fingers in half a dozen financial pies."

"How messy!" Paul chuckled and was rewarded with a heavy cuff on the ear.

Fair Haven loomed ahead, lights blazing behind cheerful curtains and a bright, outside light showed up the orderly terraces of the garden. Specimen trees on the front lawn stood out in dark relief. It was a property that could honestly be described by the house agents as 'desirable.' Its opulence was

61

obvious, even in the dark.

"Writing must be a prosperous occupation," Liz murmured, "or else he was previously a man of means."

"You must admit it hasn't gone to his head," David pointed out. "He's ordinary enough to talk to, in spite of his means".

"All the same, it's a wonder he doesn't carpet his drive, isn't it?" she whispered as they went in at the gate. Paul and Alan laughed, but Liz was conscious of David's frown and wished she had not spoken the last thought aloud.

"Why shouldn't he spend his money if he wants to instead of piling it up in a bank?" he demanded. "Others will have just as much money, but we can't read their bank balances on their faces."

"Sorry I spoke. I was joking, not meaning to be critical," Liz replied contritely.

Soon they were standing in the wide arc of light at the front door. David pressed his finger on the little illuminated button and tinkling notes sounded inside. Then they heard someone approaching the door. Dr. Mason flung the door wide. He looked at the four of them in surprise, for it was not often they had all visited him together, then held up his hands in mock alarm and said, "Help! Go away! How can I get on with my Magnum Opus with all these interruptions?" But he was smiling as he opened the door wider and stood back, inviting them inside.

Dr. Mason closed the door and the quartette

followed him across the thickly carpeted hall. He did not wait for them to explain the reason for their visit but led them straight into his study, where he had clearly been working. The room was very warm and they sank into the soft cushions when he invited them, with a wave of his hand, to sit. He himself pushed away a small table on which there was a typewriter and numerous sheets of paper, then spread himself on the chair that had been beside it. He was a man of medium height, mid-brown hair and had a pleasant face which oozed geniality, and they immediately felt at ease, even though conscious that they were about to take up his time.

"I'm sorry if we are interrupting . . . " David began but Dr. Mason laughed.

"Many great works have been written in broken or borrowed time," he told them, "So I'm sure mine will survive a break."

"All the same, if you would rather we came back another time . . . "

"To tell you the truth, I am glad of the excuse to put down my pen. Perhaps it will come easier when I go back to it."

The younger people glanced at each other, wondering who should speak and where to begin, while Dr. Mason sat with one quizzically raised eyebrow looking from one to the other and intrigued by their hesitation and unusual solemnity.

"I hope you haven't been before," he murmured

in order to encourage conversation. "I've had a couple of days away seeing my publisher."

David shook his head. "No, we haven't," he replied. "We really ought to have telephoned to see if . . . the thing is, it's rather urgent. We want . . . we need advice and we all thought you might be able to help."

"I gathered it wasn't just a social call," Dr. Mason observed dryly.

"It's about Christopher . . . "

"Christopher!" Dr. Mason took up a half smoked cigarette from the fireplace and relit it. "I thought," he said slowly, "that he was accepting his unfortunate trouble very well. He's not ill?"

"He's alright that way — I mean, he's not ill," Liz replied for her brother. "But we feel we have got to try to help him. We know he didn't do what . . . what he's supposed to have done, and we have thought of one way of doing something."

"Yes?" Dr. Mason leaned forward, serious eyes on the earnest girl.

"We talked and talked last night and went round in circles until we came up with this. It was really Alan who led us on to our present track."

Alan flushed slightly and opened his mouth to speak, but David got in first.

"We are not interested in alternative suspects," he explained emphatically, "so much as exonerating Christopher. And that is what this idea of ours seeks to do." Then he explained their plans to the attentive older man. Liz could see the doubt on Dr.

64

Mason's face as he made sure he had got the picture right, frequently interrupting to question or to make his own observations.

"Yes, I see your point," he said when the little group fell silent, awaiting his vedict.

"And you will help us?"

Dr. Mason did not answer that question straight away, but asked one himself. "You do realise what a long shot it would be, don't you?"

"Yes, but . . . "

"How many Tonys do you think there are in this district? And he might not live in this district at all. So we're thinking of how many Tonys there are in the whole country! Then, to find that one needle in the proverbial haystack, we would have to hit upon the one newspaper that he reads — most people read only one — and there are just about as many different papers in this country as Tonys!"

Dr. Mason saw that his words were having little effect upon his hearers. Each face showed grim determination, determination that only increased as he went on. He sighed slightly as he continued. "I don't want to disappoint you," he went on earnestly, "but imagine we did happen to select the correct paper. The chances of this chap's seeing the two or three lines of small type in the personal column would be little more than slight. It would be an amazing thing if such an advert produced any positive result."

"But people *do* put appeals in the personal columns," Liz objected passionately, "and I'm sure they sometimes produce results."

"Other people could see them and tell the person concerned," Alan added.

Paul stepped in front of Dr. Mason. "Please help us," he pleaded, with large, appealing eyes.

Dr. Mason placed a hand on his shoulder. "I thought you would have sorted the case out before now, P.C. Ransom," he teased.

Liz gestured impatiently. "It's just the remote possibility that it *might* work! At least we'd know we'd tried. You don't blame us for wanting to help Christopher, do you, Dr. Mason?"

"I don't blame you at all, Liz," he replied quietly, "and I think you are being very sensible about it. Not only that, but I think your suggestion is a good one, so long as you don't build your hopes up too high. I had to make sure you saw the difficulties.

"Then you will help us — regarding the wording, the different papers, and so on?" Liz pressed eagerly.

"If Pastor Meyer is happy about it, I don't see why I shouldn't be," the other man continued in the same quiet tone.

They shuffled slightly, and Liz looked down.

"So! He doesn't know?"

Liz looked pleadingly into Dr. Mason's face. "Can't you see," she said, "just what a disappointment it would be to them if nothing came of it? It would be to us, but even more to them. You've just stressed to us what a long shot it would be. They've gone through so much. They might also think we would get into trouble by raking things up, forbidding us to do anything at all. Honestly, we had thought of discussing it with them, but we didn't want to give them either vain hopes or further worries."

"And your father, David?"

"He is away for another week, yet," David replied, "but I can't really imagine his objecting to what we are proposing to do. What harm could it do?"

"And if I told you I thought you would be wasting your time and advised against it?"

"You have, more or less!" Liz cried hotly. "But it would make no difference. We are going ahead, even if we have to work out the details ourselves."

Dr. Mason sat with his finger tips together, staring thoughtfully into space. The tick of the big, brass clock sounded suddenly very loud.

"You will need to put your advertisement in both local papers," he said at length. "In spite of the possibility otherwise, the chances are that he is a local man."

"We thought he might not be a local person," David ventured hesitantly. "You see, all the fuss and publicity of the trial would surely have brought him forward if he'd known about it."

"Unless he did not care to get involved — which is another possibility," Dr. Mason pointed out. "Anyway, I can see you have been thinking it out well, so we'll get down to details."

"Oh, thank you for helping us!" Liz cried

impetuously as Dr. Mason pulled his table back, selected a clean piece of paper and a pen, and she thought how right David was in his estimation of this man. "We're ever so grateful."

"Call it my contribution towards a good cause," Dr. Mason replied. "As long as you keep me informed of developments. That is my one condition. I'm as anxious as you to know what will happen. And as chief adviser, I'm involving myself in a major criminal case, whether I like it or not."

It took only a few minutes to produce the list they wanted, then Dr. Mason asked to see the rough advertisement they had written. After reading it through, he made only minor alterations, and handed it back.

"That should be quite adequate," he said. "It will cost you a fortune if you try to say too much. It will be enough as it is! Incidentally, who's footing the bill?" The bantering tone had returned to his voice.

They smiled and said in the same tone that they'd manage it between them if they raided their piggy banks.

"Well, you know where to come if it doesn't stretch quite far enough," the doctor said magnanimously. "Now tell me how your brother is."

They talked about Christopher for a while, then Dr. Mason asked about his flat.

"Then I've probably missed my chance," he said on being told that Christopher was giving it up. "I've never been inside it. Your brother invited me often enough and I had every intention of calling, sometime. You know," he added confidentially to Liz, "that brother of yours must have hidden talents. I wonder how he solved all Tony's problems in such a short time that night, or what advice he gave him."

"He no doubt told him what Dad would have told him," Liz answered without hesitation, " that he needed a compass and an anchor on the troubled seas of life. He would warn him of sin and tell him of salvation."

"I would have thought that was calculated to make him more depressed than ever," Dr. Mason said with a laugh. "All that talk of sin and guilt, heaven and hell! However, if it did the trick . . . Now, perhaps one of you could explain a phenomenon."

Four pairs of eyes gazed at him, puzzled. Liz's face was flushed in her annoyance at his disdain of spiritual matters.

He laughed again. "It isn't anything strange not to hear Alan's voice for an hour or so," he said winking in the fair lad's direction, "but I've never known Paul to be so quiet before. It really is a marvellous treat, but something tells me he'll make up for it another time!"

"I've decided to be like the wise old owl," Paul replied, his eyes round and guileless.

They prepared to leave, once again assuring Dr. Mason, in reply to his insistent reminder, that they would let him know if and when anything happened.

"Remember," he said on the doorstep. "Don't set your hopes too high, in case you are disappointed. Still, coincidences do happen. So good luck."

Neither Liz nor the two younger boys believed in either coincidence or luck as determining forces, but they did not think it the time or place to take the point up, and David was thanking Dr. Mason profusely.

Back at the Ransoms' home, Paul was sent off to bed before Aunty Janet appeared to do it, then the others got down to writing the necessary letters to the various newspapers selected, enclosing their article for publication. The advertisement was to be a straight forward SOS for the Tony who recognised himself from the few items of description stated to get in touch with them immediately. The Ransoms' phone number was supplied.

"We'd better add 'Evenings only'," David said. "For there is no-one at home during the day."

Once they were ready, David gathered up the envelopes, promising to get them in the next morning's post, and put them in his pocket.

"That's a good job done, thanks to Dr. Mason," he said in a satisfied voice. "Now, until something happens, there is nothing we can do but wait."

Chapter 6

Paul, however, had other ideas. There was plenty to do, and he wasted none of his available time. He resented the fact that school, homework and housework accounted for all but about two hours of every day. However, he could stretch those two hours into three or even four by spending his bus journeys, the times he lay awake in bed, and even parts of selected boring lessons, deep in thought. And he had all day on Saturdays.

His first priority was to get his notes and observations up to date. He felt this was important as it helped to fix the details in his mind and would, in theory, show up any flaws the more clearly when he saw them in black and white. He poured over his notebook for long periods at a time, willing some solution to show itself and waiting for some flash of inspiration, then replaced it under his mattress where he kept it for safety. In the meantime, there were investigations he could carry out. He was not at all clear about what he would do with any findings he might come up with — probably simply refer them to the others when they proved sufficiently stunning! He had no intention of being deliberately secretive for very long or of doing anything precipitately in what he considered his own specialised field, for he had no desire to bring the ire and disdain of his brother upon himself. The button which he carefully guarded occasionally gave him a twinge of conscience and several times he almost brought it out to show the others. But not quite. He could apply a few simple tests easily enough himself, no doubt saving a lot of needless debate as to what to do with it. Anyway, it would probably turn out that it was not pertinent to the case at all.

The next thing he did after writing up his notes was to write a letter. It was to Christopher and he wrote four pages of general chatter without a mention of what they were doing on his behalf. He had more sense than to do that off his own bat. But he did fix the precious button carefully to the bottom of the letter with sellotape and add a P.S.

"Found this button," he stated vaguely, "and as it isn't ours, thought it must belong to you."

It didn't matter where Christopher thought he had found it. Probably he would assume that Paul meant it had been found in the Ransoms' home, as the writer preferred him to think. Paul was sure the button did not belong to Christopher, but he

72

wanted to know if he recognised it. It was no use his following the matter up if there was no mystery about it in the first place.

It was too early for their advertisement to be in any of the papers that evening, so David felt it safe to go out. At Paul's suggestion, they went over to the manse. His brother did not need any persuading, for David gave the impression that he was eager to find out if there had been any new thoughts on matters so far. Paul also had an idea that Liz was another reason David was glad to go. He had noticed the 'soppy' way he looked at her sometimes.

Mrs. Meyer was busy in the kitchen and looked very tired, although she greeted the Ransom brothers heartily enough. Pastor Meyer was getting ready to go and see Christopher. This was the foreseen possibility that Paul had hoped for, and he had brought his letter with him. He took it from his pocket and held it out towards Christopher's father.

"I've just written to Christopher," he said. "Could you please . . . ?" He caught David's worried glance and shook his head ever so slightly. His brother seemed to be reassured, for he relaxed and turned to speak to Mrs. Meyer. " . . . It would save me postage if you would take it."

Pastor Meyer laughed and said he would, though he would expect a bit of commission.

Paul didn't really understand that but, as it was obviously intended as a joke, he smiled himself and thanked Christopher's father.

The young people didn't get much chance to talk to each other, for Liz was helping her mother with household jobs and Alan was in his own room toiling over an especially heavy load of homework. Liz looked much happier tonight, almost as bright as before the coming of the family trouble. Her mother kept glancing at her in surpise, as if trying to account for the sudden change.

They talked generalities for the most part, school, work, the neighbourhood and how David and Paul were coping without their parents.

"Oh, I manage him very well," said Paul, grinning at his brother, "but he will *not* go to bed on a night!"

The remark caused amusement, for they all knew the truth of the matter.

Apart from this frivolous remark, Paul had very little to say. Neither did he seem to be listening very closely to other people's conversations. David, aware of danger signals when his brother was quiet, wondered what was on his mind. Definitely not the French verbs he by right ought to have been learning that evening!

"I wish we had as many photographs as you have," Paul cried suddenly, glancing through the open door into the sitting room where the piano top and the wall behind were liberally decorated with them. "Family ones, I mean — you know, with everyone from childhood upwards."

"Oh, we've a lot more than you can see there," Mrs. Meyer told him. "Bring him some of the albums to look through, Liz.''

David frowned. He had never noticed any such lack in his family picture gallery.

Paul sat with his eyes glued to the glossy pages, occasionally interrupting the conversation with eager questions. ''Is this when you got married, Mrs. Meyer? or ''Is this Alan when he was a baby?'' or ''How long is it since this one was taken?'' Liz kept one eye on the album while she worked, and frequently broke off to describe some humourous background to a photograph or tell Paul who certain people were, so that before long Paul did not need to ask any questions.

''Come on, we'll have to go now,'' David told him eventually. ''We're later than we should be already.''

''Just this last album,'' pleaded Paul with something like desperation in his tone and the Meyers were amused at his intense interest in the pictures. He turned to an enlargement of a family wedding photograph, and his eyes gleamed as he looked down. There appeared to be a fairly wide representation of the Meyer family featured on it.

''That's a wedding photograph of a cousin of mine,'' Liz explained, having herself become engrossed and having finally abandoned the job she was supposed to be doing. ''My cousin, Susan Barrett. She married a man much older than herself, as you can see. And that,'' she said pointing, ''is . . . is her brother, John Barrett.'' Liz dare not lift her eyes to meet David's, but she was conscious of his

75

sudden interest in the picture. She went on quickly, "Then, to the left is Grandad Meyer and . . . " Liz continued all round the group of people, but Paul's eyes had lingered on John Barrett, though he murmured in response in all the right places when Liz moved on to another person.

At this point, the door opened and Pastor Meyer entered. David got up to go, pulling at Paul's hair as he did so to raise him from his chair.

"Christopher is in remarkable form," Pastor Meyer told them all brightly. "Really, I'm bound to admit that this affair has been a blessing in disguise in Christopher's case. He's thinking of starting taking a Bible Correspondence Course while he has plenty of time! Then he is considering taking up full time christian work after he's . . . afterwards. Oh, and he gave me this for you," he said returning Paul's envelope to him. "I think it is just a note to say he will write later!"

David would not allow Paul to look at any more photographs, but his brother had seen what he wanted to see and left happily enough.

"Now! What are you up to, rascal?" David demanded as soon as they were on their own, "and why the sudden interest in family snapshots?"

"Maybe I've decided to go in for photography rather than detecting," suggested his brother evasively.

"That would be quite a relief! — but, come on, out with it!"

"I . . . er . . . Well, I thought it would be as well to

know what our suspects look like," Paul replied carefully. "We — we ought to be able to recognise them, don't you think? We can all recognise Lester Addison now — I once saw him in the shop — but neither of us had ever seen John Barrett, had we? Now we would know him if we saw him. You know, just in case."

"In case what?" David demanded. "If this Tony turns up, we've no need to bother our heads chasing the real crooks. The police will take care of that."

Paul's eyes gleamed again but it was too dark for David to notice, or he would have issued a very strong word of warning to his eager, young brother. As it was, he just said, "Well, I don't want you getting into mischief, so watch it!"

Arriving at home, Paul was not reluctant for once to go up to his room and get ready for bed. Once under the covers, he took out the envelope from Christopher and extracted the brief note.

'Thanks a lot for letter,' he read. 'Will read it later and reply. However, read your P.S. but return the button, as it is not mine. Never seen it before that I know of. Don't go in for such flamboyance!"

Satisfied with the evening's events, Paul placed the precious button in a safe place, then put out the light and was asleep in a few minutes. Aunty Janet could come and kiss him good night for all he cared!

The next day was Saturday. David had to go into work. It was unusual for him to be needed at the weekend but his firm had a backlog of work at the moment and was eager to get up to date — hence overtime for a reluctant David. This suited Paul's purpose very well as he did not want his time monopolising, but to go out on his own private business. Perhaps it should be added that Paul, knowing his own inadequacy, deliberately lingered before he set out to commend his ways to his Heavenly Father. Since he became a christian he, perhaps more than any of them, realised the necessity of relating every detail of his life to the central hub of his faith in Christ.

He set off confidently, going into Town on his bike. There, he did some shopping — as much as his pocket money would allow, a comic, a detective paper-back and a set of felt pens. These all fitted perfectly in his pockets. The bulges did nothing for his figure, but what were pockets for?

It was approaching lunch time when Paul came to Raynor's jewellers where Christopher had worked until recently. There, Paul leaned his bicycle against the wall and took the familiar wheel-like button from the handkerchief where he had it tied in a corner and placed it on the ground in the shop doorway close to the glass window. He put it carefully upside down so that it would not be very noticeable. Then he stood staring in the shop window as if trying to decide which gold watch he should buy! He stood there for ten minutes. He could not be seen from inside the shop, so he did not mind waiting. For another ten minutes he stood, seeing the door open and shut many times as customers went in and out of the shop.

The door opened again and a youth with red hair came out. Paul did not need telling that this was no customer but the person he had been waiting for. Lester Addison did not look to his left hand or right but walked straight away in the same direction as Liz and David had recently seen him go.

Paul did not hesitate. Hurriedly picking up the button from the doorway, he ran after the other and tapped him on the arm.

"Excuse me," he panted. "Did you drop this? I saw you come out of the shop just now and this was in the doorway." He held out the button, now the right way up.

Lester Addison glanced at it for not more than a second, then started to walk away again.

"It's not mine," he said over his shoulder. "I've never seen it before."

Paul smiled at the receding figure and replaced the button carefully in the same grubby corner of handkerchief.

Now he had a rather longer journey to make. Getting on his bicycle, he worked out the route in his head and prepared to leave the town on the eastern side. He knew from a casual remark made by Liz the name of the village where John Barrett lived, though not his address. He would just have to risk enquiring for him when he got there. He knew that it was only a small village and Liz had said that he'd lived there all his life, so everyone should know where he lived.

He halted at the traffic lights and then rode on again in the stream of vehicles going his way. He was accustomed to riding in town and soon found himself safely through, in spite of the congestion caused by football fans on their way to the local grounds.

Half an hour later, he reached the village he sought. It consisted of a centrally placed church with a square tower, surrounded by a cluster of grey houses giving the impression of a bunch of children clinging to their mother's skirts, Paul thought. A few more isolated houses stood further back, larger houses with more foliage around them.

Paul got off his bike and walked it across to where an elderly man was putting a white envelope into the red letter box on the front of the Post Office. Drawing level, he asked where John Barrett lived.

"John Barrett, young man? Yes. The house down the left hand fork in the road with blue shutters and white paintwork. There is only one. Church View, it's called."

Paul thanked him and pedalled away thinking in amusement that the way the man had said it made it sound as if it was the road that had blue shutters and white paintwork. He reflected that his English teacher's lessons on qualifying phrases must be bearing fruit in his brain at last!

Church View was a semi-detached house down a short lane bordered by high hedges. There appeared to be no-one about. Paul hoped he had not come on a wild goose chase, for he would not be able to come again until the following Saturday — if he could wangle it then. However he had plenty of time so all he could do was wait. Paul was not wanting in patience, sometimes termed stubbornness by those who wanted to criticise!

Opposite was a gate into a field. Paul dismounted and leaned his bike against this gate. Once more he took out the handkerchief and removed the button, placing it this time on the road close to the gate of Church View, upside down as before. The gate into the field was not in sight from the house, so Paul now took out his comic, climbed to the top of the gate and sat reading, facing the road. While he read, he was also thinking. John Barrett might not be at home. He might go out in a car or come home in a car and not linger at the gate, letting a passenger open and close it. John Barrett was not bound to go out or come in at all. But if he was engaged to be married, Paul told himself that Saturday afternoon was as likely a time as any for the couple to be going out somewhere. He was reasonably sure that he would recognise him. It was cold and Paul hoped that he would soon appear. The thoughts of sitting there all afternoon were rather daunting.

As if having read his thoughts, a figure appeared behind the garden gate clad in rough jacket and gardening gloves. He leaned over his own gate for a moment, staring at the boy opposite intent on his comic. Then he took up a spade and began to dig, still within sight. It was undoubtedly John Barrett. Paul recognised him from the photograph he had seen. It was quite clear that he had no plans for going out. Paul, his eyes still on his book, tried to work out what to do. In the end, John Barrett helped him out.

"Hey, you," he called across, coming back to the gate. "I hope you're not going to get up to any mischief."

Paul realised that it was nearly the beginning of November, the time when little boys specialise in the pursuit of mischief! He jumped off the gate and walked across the road, turning his roundest bluest eyes on the man standing watching him from behind the garden gate.

"Oh, no," he assured him with the smile most people found hard to resist. "I've just cycled quite a long way and was having a bit of a rest before I went on. I'm making for the town. Do you know how far it is? Will I be able to do it in half an hour?"

The suspicion had left John Barrett's face and he assured the boy that a half hour should be quite sufficient. Then he saw the lad in front of him suddenly spot something on the ground near his gate, stoop to pick it up then offer it to him.

"Have you lost a button?" Paul asked innocently. "It's an unusual one."

John Barrett took it and stared hard at it.

"Very unusual," he agreed, "but not my style. Never seen it before," he said like the other two before him. "It doesn't belong to anyone in this house." He would have thrown it down again had not Paul held out his hand for it. "Anyway, you turn right at the church on to the main road, and it will take you straight to Town."

"Oh, well, I'd better go now," Paul said, stuffing button and comic hurriedly into his pocket and going to retrieve his bicycle. "Bye. Thanks for the directions."

Paul was a little disappointed as he set off back the way that he had come but at the same time he was glad that he'd been able to apply his test to both of their suspects. So the button did not belong to either of them, he thought, pedalling hard to cover the ground as quickly as he could. That meant that there was still no evidence that either of them had been in Christopher's flat in recent days. It was disappointing but it did not make any difference to their suspicions regarding the two men. The motives were still there. After all, the button probably was not incriminating evidence. It could quite well have belonged to an innocent party, Christopher's neighbour, his meter reader, or to his newspaper boy!

Chapter 7

On Monday, the first of the advertisements appeared in the papers. David had to search hard to find any of them and the others were shocked to see the insignificant two lines of theirs apparently lost in a sea of print.

"If Tony does happen to get hold of any of these papers he'll never see that!" Liz cried in despair. "And to think what it's cost!"

"Yes, well, Dr. Mason warned us it would be a long shot," David reminded her. "What did you expect — six inches on the front page?"

Alan looked at his sister and said quietly, "I think we should trust God rather than the size of the advert."

David sighed impatiently. "I notice it was Dr. Mason you had to go to for help the other day," he said provocatively.

Liz turned on him angrily. "Every morning we

84

commit the day to God," she informed him abruptly, "and that covers every event and every conversation. Alan's right, and I'm sorry I was despondent."

David put his hands in front of his face as if to ward off blows, then changed the subject by asking if Paul had finished his homework.

"Yes, Dad," Paul replied cheekily.

It was evening and they were at the Ransoms' house, all of them inclined to feel nervous and pessimistic. Until they opened the newspapers they had somehow expected the phone to ring the moment the advert appeared but now that the time had come and they had seen the size of the advert it seemed less likely. David's private opinion was that it wouldn't ring at all, at least not to announce a mystery Tony. In fact, the telephone did ring twice that first evening of waiting. Each time, they looked at each other, feeling apprehensive about answering it, but the first time it was Mrs. Ransom making sure that all was well at home, and the second time it was a wrong number.

"Let's play Scrabble," Paul suggested.

"I couldn't concentrate," Liz objected.

"It would be better than just sitting waiting," Alan said eagerly, glad of any possible diversion, and Paul went to fetch the box.

Liz and David both joined in rather reluctantly. Liz felt too strung up, but had the wisdom to realise that a game might help. She would have preferred a physical scrap with any takers, though, rather than mental concentration without the physical exertion. For his part, David, as the eldest of them, was conscious of the sudden responsibilities weighing heavily upon him, so that a game seemed too trivial a thing to consider. David regarded himself as decidedly adult but he nevertheless at this time wished his parents had been at home to advise them. All the same, he pondered, they probably could not have done any more than Dr. Mason had done — no doubt less, for they most likely knew little more than David about respective newspapers.

"Come on, David. It's your go." A voice broke into his thoughts and he put down the first word that came into his head.

In between turns, David tried to work out what he would say if the man Tony did ring up. It was better to decide now, so that he could explain coherently when it happened.

Then he began to wonder what they would do if Tony did not answer their advertisement. It would mean that they were back to square one but Liz, he knew, would not want to leave it at that and abandon the case.

"You can't have *onto*," Paul informed Alan as he put four of his tiles down on the board. "Our teacher said that *on* and *to* were two different words."

"Rubbish! Course I can have it!" Alan objected emphatically. "*Upon* is a word and so is *into* so, why shouldn't *onto* be a word, as well? It's right, isn't it, David?"

"What? I suppose so. Oh, I don't know." David was not really interested in the intricacies of spelling at the moment. They could have what they liked for him. He felt so unsettled and somehow inadequate. Most of all, he was impatient for something to happen, even while at the same time not expecting it to. He would be relieved when the whole episode was over, whether or not Christopher was freed as a result. Whether or not Christopher was freed . . . His face flushed slightly when he recognised the selfishness of his sentiments. He knew that his own comfort and mental ease were more important to him than Christopher's reputation and release. He admitted it honestly, albeit to himself, and in that moment of revelation he recognised that that made him different from the others, whose whole concern was for Christopher. But Christopher was alright, he argued — Pastor Meyer had said so. In fact he had implied that he was actually benefiting from the situation. David told himself that his attitude was a reasonable one. Why shouldn't he live primarily for himself? No-one else would care for his interests. He would not feel it encumbent on others to put him first, so why should he . . . ? Liz would not like his philosophy, he knew. She would say, as he had heard her father say more than once from the pulpit, that the christian's obligation was to live to God first, then for others, and only then for oneself. But he wasn't a christian by their definition. He had his own definition, but that was not based upon the example of the Son of God giving Himself for the salvation of others. Those were primitive ideas of a former age, unsuited to his concept of the dignity of man.

"It's in the dictionary," Alan exulted, closing the deciding volume with a snap.

"Well, it shouldn't be, then," Paul grumbled unyieldingly. "It makes a mockery of Mrs. Price's lessons. She must have got her facts somewhere. Anyway, we let you have it, didn't we? It's your turn, David."

"When Tony rings," Liz interrupted with emphasis on the word 'when', "do we ask him to call here?"

"Yes, even if he lives in Glasgow," Paul could not resist saying.

"If he lives pretty near, yes," David replied, ignoring his brother. "It would be better than talking on the phone. Either that or go to see him — but it would be difficult for us to travel any day but Saturday."

But the telephone remained depressingly silent.

"If Tony doesn't ring tonight, there are two more chances," Liz consoled them all. "We ought to have put the advert in for a week, instead of three days."

"We couldn't have afforded," David pointed out.

"It's your turn," Paul patiently informed his brother again with a slight nudge. "I'm beating you tonight. I've got 140 so far and you have only 98!"

"Enjoy your glory, Junior. It won't happen again!" David promised.

The evening dragged by, minute by measured minute. Sometimes they talked, sometimes they just thought, but always they waited and listened.

"I've just had a thought," Alan said suddenly once over. "We're expecting this chap Tony to see the advert. If he can see it, so can anyone else."

"Anyone else?"

Liz understood. "Oh, no! You're right, Alan. I hadn't thought of that. Anyone might see it, the neighbours, people at church — which ultimately means Mum and Dad! They could easily get to know — even if they don't see the advert themselves."

"Does it matter?" David asked.

"It doesn't matter in one way, but you know very well that I wanted it to be a fait accompli," Liz wailed. "I'd hate their hopes to be raised just to be dashed again. We . . . ."

"Your turn, Liz."

"Well, it can't be helped," David told her, silently indicating with his finger a convenient space to insert several of her letters. "That aspect is out of our control. We'll just have to hope for the best — I *told* you what to put down. That's no good. *Supply* has two p's in it. I thought you would be able to spell better than that, Elizabeth Meyer."

"I know it has, but I did tell you I wouldn't be able to concentrate tonight."

"Do you think your father would be angry?"

"No, I don't but that's not what I'm worried about, anyway, as I've just explained. It's the

89

emotional involvement."

"I think we should tell them," Alan suggested. "It would be better than that they should hear from someone else."

"No. Let's wait a day or two at least."

"I don't see why we shouldn't wait," David agreed. "It's only what we decided and we are doing no harm. I agree that it would be ideal for Pastor and Mrs. Meyer not to know about it until afterward, if it were possible. We just can't help it if they do hear in the meantime."

"Why doesn't this Tony chap ring?" Paul asked almost fiercely.

"I don't expect him tonight. It's too soon," David said "It'll be a wonder if we hear tomorrow, either."

"If he's going to come forward at all, why didn't he show his face when the case was on?" Alan wondered aloud. "I would have thought he was more likely to have seen all the rigmarole in the papers then than our small piece."

"Thanks for those encouraging words!"

"There's another thing," Liz sighed. "Do you think the police will listen to him *when* he turns up, if he's just a down and out?"

"Who said he was a down and out?" David demanded.

"Well, I got the impression . . . Christopher . . ."

"Being in trouble doesn't necessarily make him a hobo," he replied. "He might be, of course. But the police will listen to him whoever he is, provided his story is convincing enough."

"I wish he would come, yet I'm scared of him coming, at the same time," Liz groaned. "He might be in trouble again — whatever trouble it is — in spite of what Christopher did for him. He might even be drunk!"

Scrabble was forgotten for the moment. Paul looked up suddenly.

"I bet I know the reason for Tony's silence. He was probably in trouble with the police already — that's why he chose not to get involved, but it's a fine way of repaying Christopher! We never thought of that kind of trouble. No wonder Christopher refused to discuss his problems!"

"Hey, steady! You're only guessing!"

"If that's true, we're wasting our time sitting here waiting for the phone to ring," Liz concluded. "I don't think I like this Tony."

"I'm probably wrong," Paul conceded. "And I'll protect you when he comes."

But Liz was not in the mood for joking. The others weren't either.

"Come on," David urged them. "Finish this most fascinating game. It's time Paul was thinking about bed."

Paul grimaced.

"Yes, and we must go. We promised Mum we wouldn't be late."

Alan won the game but nobody noticed, much to his chagrin for it didn't happen very often. David set off with them towards the manse, once he had seen Paul disappear upstairs. His intention was to walk as far as the crossroads and then return. It was only a few minutes' walk away, but he gave Paul instructions as to what to say if the expected call came during that time.

The night was inclined to be foggy again. They did not loiter. There was no point. The telephone call they all wanted had not come. What they desired now was for tomorrow evening to come as quickly as possible, and with it new hope.

Still within sight of the Ransoms' home, they reached the crossroads. A car with only parking lights was drawn in close to the curb. Two figures were dimly visible inside.

"That's funny," Liz said. "I'm sure that car was there when we came. That's hours ago."

"Courting couple," Alan grinned as if he knew all about that kind of thing.

"Can't see very well now, but I thought before that they were a couple of men," Liz argued. "I don't suppose I would have taken much notice, but I thought it was a funny place to stop. The road is so narrow and the car is blocking up that entrance."

"Anyway, it's nothing to do with us," David replied a little impatiently. "See you tomorrow night."

The telephone rang as David walked in at the front door. His pulses began to race as he hurried to answer it, but it was only Dr. Mason inquiring how the first evening had gone.

"No success, I'm afraid, Dr. Mason," David replied. "But there are still two chances."

"Exactly. Exactly. Remember — you'll let me know?"

"Straight away," promised David. "We won't forget. And thank you."

The intervening day seemed interminable to them all. They tried working especially hard in their various spheres, they tried deliberately thinking of other things, they tried to tell themselves philosophically that in twenty years' time today would be forgotten, but the hands of the clock went round no more quickly. Liz, at school, felt to be living in unreality. She was not sure which were the more unreal, the world of arts and sciences or the slightly nightmarish periods of waiting, waiting, like last evening and this coming evening . . .

During that day she developed a sense of foreboding which she could not explain. As if something was wrong. Something did not add up. She was annoyed with herself for it was an illogical foreboding. There was nothing tangible to account for it. Nothing was any different from what it had been. Perhaps behind it all was her fear that the man Tony would not turn up, that they were not going to be able to do anything to help Christopher, after all. No, Liz was sure there was something else worrying her, something she ought to be able to put her finger on. Perhaps they were on the wrong track, somehow. For one moment of panic she was sure they had worked everything out wrongly, that Tony had been a fake sent to keep Christopher occupied that fateful night, or some such thing.

Unseen forces were arrayed against them. Grimly she drew the reins on the unreasonable thoughts that were running away with her. They could not be wrong in their conclusions that someone had a grudge against Christopher, whether it were Lester Addison, John Barrett or somebody they had not thought of. She must concentrate on facts, not intangible feelings or fancies. There were plenty of perplexing aspects, but what they were seeking to do was surely simple enough, seeking the one person able to prove Christopher's story. If and when he appeared, the whole thing was over as far as they were concerned. So why was she allowing herself to get into such a state?

Nevertheless, she was shivering when she and Alan reached the Ransoms' house that evening, not because of the cold, but with nervous tension. It did not help that the car they had seen the previous evening was there again, not in quite the same place but not many yards away, inconspicuously parked in the deep gloom on the outer side of a tall garden hedge. It was too dark to see if it had any occupants.

"Why shouldn't it be there?" David objected when she told him of its presence again. "I don't know the people in the houses just there, but it probably belongs to one of them."

"If it did, they would surely take it into the drive. And it was outside a different house last night." Liz seemed determined to make a mystery out of it. "Besides, they wouldn't have sat in the car all that time last evening if they lived at the house."

"You don't seriously think someone was sitting in the car all the time you were here last night!" David cried incredulously. "Honestly, Liz, what's got into you? Why would they do that? Not only was it dark and misty, but that corner's not exactly a scenic viewpoint!"

They declined Paul's offer to bring out the Scrabble again. Liz and Alan had both brought homework with them, and David simply refused to play. He did not feel as keyed up tonight for he did not expect their phone call — not yet, at any rate. His thoughts during the day had convinced him that if it did eventually come, it would probably be in a week's time, or two or even three, when someone perhaps lighting his fire accidentally caught sight of those two insignificant lines . . .

The telephone rang and Paul ran through to answer it.

"It'll be Andrew Hardy," he called over his shoulder. "He said he would ring to let me know if he could go to the football match on Saturday."

A few seconds later he was back, an awed look on his face.

"For you, David — or Liz. It's him. Tony."

"You," Liz whispered hoarsely.

David went out hesitantly and they heard him speak but could not catch the words.

The three stood in stunned silence, surprised by the suddenness of the call. David was back before any of them spoke or moved.

He grinned at their strained, apprehensive faces.

"He lives only about three miles away on the other side of Town, believe it or not," he told them, a note of excitement in his voice which broke the spell. "He didn't know about Christopher's trial because he has been out of the country. He was quite shocked."

"You weren't talking long. Is he . . . is he . . . ?"

David's eyes were gleaming. "His car's out of action," he said, "but he is going to get a bus and come round here straight away. He says he will gladly do all he can to help."

Liz sat down, suddenly exhausted. Paul did a frenzied war dance round the settee and Alan and David stood there at a bit of a loss to know what to do but smiling all over their faces. It was all over. They had won. Liz now felt ashamed of her fears of the afternoon and ready to cry with relief.

Paul collapsed in a heap at Liz's feet. "Oh dear!" he groaned. "It will take him at least half an hour to get here. He'll have to get a bus, then there's the journey, and he'll have to walk from our stop." He looked at his watch, calculating. "There is a bus gets to the road end in exactly twenty five and a half minutes. How can we *exist* all that time?"

They all felt the same. Liz laughed, starry eyed. "If we all start to bite our fingernails, they should just about be chewed away by the time he is due to arrive!" She looked doubtfully at David. "You told him *exactly* how to find us, didn't you?"

"I gave him every detail — down to the colour of our eyes," he replied frivolously. "You could have

96

spoken to him if you'd wanted."

Liz shuddered. "I didn't want to," she admitted. "What . . . what did he sound like?"

"Pleasant. Cultured. Authoritative, but easy enough to talk to," David told her. "If he's a hobo, he's the best spoken one I've ever heard!"

They wandered aimlessly about and David brought some toffees out to chew instead of their finger nails.

"I think we should give Dr. Mason a ring while we are waiting," he suggested suddenly. "He helped us no end and we did promise to let him know as soon as anything happened."

"Good idea," cried Liz, springing up. "That will account for another minute or two. Come on! What are we waiting for?"

David made the call. Dr. Mason lifted the receiver almost immediately.

"Dr. Mason? David speaking. You'll be interested to know that Tony has turned up! He didn't know about Christopher because he's been abroad. He's on his way here this very minute, and he's going to do all he can for us."

There was a brief silence as if Dr. Mason was quite stunned and David grinned, then the voice said, "Well, well, well! I never expected it, I must admit. It seemed an impossible chance. The gods must be on your side! You don't know how lucky you have been. But you deserve a break, after all your effort. Christopher will be proud of you — as he should be with such loyal allies."

"Oh, it's partly thanks to you. We felt a bit helpless before coming to you."

"That was nothing. The least I could do. Writing is my business, after all." Then he wanted to know all the details, where the man came from, what his other name was and how he was travelling.

David answered his first and last question, then added, "His surname is Masterson — but we'll no doubt know more about him in a short while."

"Oh, well, I'm delighted for you. Thanks for letting me know so soon. I've no plans for going away in the immediate future, so keep in touch.

"We are fortunate it has happened just now," David told him, "when you are at home. Anyway, we'll let you know what he says."

"Great!" Dr. Mason exclaimed. "Not long now and you will be able to kill the fatted calf!"

"I wonder where he goes when he is away." Paul pondered after they had rung off.

"On business, I expect, nosy!" was his brother's rejoinder.

"Or to one of his sunshine homes," Liz suggested. "He'll have to spend enough time at them to make it worth while keeping them."

"Must be a nice life, all that travelling and changes of scenery," was Paul's verdict, then he added, "but not as *useful* as detective work."

"Might be just as useful, for all you . . . "

David stopped when the doorbell rang. Paul was halfway to the door by the time the others moved. It was a tense moment for them all. They heard voices, then Paul returned leading a man of small stature, a man David immediately suspected of being many years younger than his head of thick, silver hair suggested. He was immaculately dressed, and that air of authority David had noticed even in his voice was something he seemed to wear with his clothes. All in all, he was obviously as far as he could be from being the 'down and out' Liz had envisaged. Taken aback and rather overawed, the young folks felt all at once tongue-tied, until they noticed the deep blue eyes set wide in an open face with a twinkle that belied the general impression of dignity he gave.

The man came into the room and it seemed full of him, in spite of his smallness. "Mr. Ransom?" he asked.

"I am David Ransom. I spoke to you on the phone," David said, stepping forward and holding out his hand with an adult dignity unconsciously seeking to match the man's own. "This is Elizabeth, Christopher's sister and Alan, his brother. Paul here is my brother. My parents are away, and it was we who put the advertisement in the newspaper."

"Well, I guess I am the man you are looking for. My name is Tony Masterson, and I see now that I should have been more forthcoming about my identity that night, as it turns out. But I think I should be able to successfully account for the night in question to those that matter. I have much to thank your dear brother for, Elizabeth, and I shall be glad to partially repay him for his kindness to me. I gathered from the phone call just now that there has been a certain amount of drama while I have been away!''

David reached over and took up a newspaper cutting from the top of the piano. ''That is the article as it was in our newspaper,'' he said, handing it over. ''All the details of the case are there and make it clearer than we would.''

Tony Masterson sat down at their invitation and began to read. His reading was punctuated by exclamations and questions.

''But this is fantastic! Really, the poor boy! Understandable, but all mistaken conclusions. I wouldn't have believed this possible!''

Only the questions expected a reply and, for the most part, the little group around him stood silently, experiencing again with him their own shock and unbelief.

''Your parents?'' Tony inquired of Liz. ''Why is it not they I am seeing?''

''They have had a great ordeal,'' Liz replied hesitantly. ''We didn't want them to have another one.'' She flushed slightly, ''It was my idea, really, to go it alone.''

Tony gazed round at them again, one by one, not revealing his thoughts, and they exchanged wary glances as he returned to the narrative. He seemed unaware of all the eyes upon him.

Paul's fingers, in his pocket, played with his handkerchief and he remembered that it was the one that held the button from Christopher's flat. He was in the habit of taking it out of its hiding place under the mattress and studying it as if it could tell him something, and he had forgotten to put it away again. He looked at Tony Masterson, his mind trying to visualise the button on his person. He admitted to himself that he couldn't. It had been unlikely on Christopher, but more so on Tony Masterson. He was conservative, spelled with capital letters, from top to toe. Paul thought he did not even need to question him, but he would see . . .

"Most peculiar," Tony summed up as he handed back the cutting. "The whole affair raises a lot of questions. If someone wanted the Hampshire diamonds, why plant them on Christopher? If, on the other hand, it was done to deliberately implicate him, why aim so high as the Hampshire diamonds to serve the purpose? Was it an isolated theft, or part of something bigger? How unfortunate that I was away! The circumstances were certainly weighed very heavily against Christopher and strongly pointed to his being an accessory to an organised gang of crooks. After all, what could he do himself with such a celebrated heirloom? However, I assure you that Christopher is quite innocent. I was with him in the flat when this must have taken place. That lets him out completely. It is quite obvious that someone must have entered his kitchen while we were talking, without our hearing them."

"And you will tell the police?" Liz asked eagerly.

"But of course," the man replied. "With the utmost of pleasure! Don't worry. I promise I will go first thing in the morning. What a difficult time it must have been for all of you. You know, I am quite shocked to think that even while Christopher was putting himself out to help me, disaster was falling upon him."

Sympathy softened his features as he surveyed them. He was not expecting an answer, but simply reflecting aloud.

Liz, conscious that he was here on her brother's account and that up to now their visitor had done nearly all the talking, decided it was time she said something.

"I can't tell you how grateful I am — we all are," she assured him warmly, her eyes shining with joy. "And Mum and Dad will be more so. What a relief it will be to live normally again, to have Christopher at home with us, and to leave it to someone else to find out who would do such a thing to him!"

"And leave off sleuthing?" Paul asked reluctantly.

Tony Masterson regarded them closely, his eyebrows raised. "Is there something you haven't told me?" he inquired.

David put up a hand to restrain his brother. "Not really. We've pondered and theorised, but all we have found are two people who might have a motive for wishing ill on Christopher."

In the pause after David had finished speaking, Tony Masterson obviously juggled with a flood of thoughts that sought utterance.

"Listen all of you," he said at last. "Take my advice. If you know anything, or suspect anyone, I urge you to tell the police. Don't get involved yourselves. This hasn't the appearance of an amateur job, and the police are probably right in considering it part of a larger spate of thefts. What amateur would steal the Hampshire diamonds? One has to have the right contacts for disposing of such items. Similarly, no-one simply intent on personal spite would go to the risk of breaking into some aristrocratic home and steal its diamonds to plant on a third person. They would surely plant some valuable of their own where the only risk was in getting that article into the victim's possession . . ."

"Oh!"

Wide eyes surveyed him.

"Have I said something?"

Liz groaned. "We hadn't thought of that. We've thought of just about everything else, I'm sure. You see, there *are* two people we know of who have rather a large grudge against Christopher, but their motives are personal ones. If you are right, they are ruled out."

Liz sighed with exasperation. "Mr. Masterson, we seem to do nothing but go round in circles."

Tony's eyes twinkled in their friendly, reassuring way. "It seems to me that you have done the one sensible thing, taken steps to find me," he replied. "And with the success of that venture, your headaches should be over. Why should you worry over who did it, as long as Christopher didn't? The police are there for that. As I said, this job bears the mark of an expert. Granted, something must have gone wrong. Take my advice," he repeated. "Tell the police, if there is anything worth telling. Otherwise forget about it. Tomorrow night at this time Christopher's troubles will be over, and that means yours, too."

Suddenly, they didn't want to think about it or talk about it any more. Only Paul experienced a brief pang of regret, but he sensibly realised that it was for the best. It was all over.

Tony got up and David jumped up after him, remembering his duties as host.

"I think Liz was just going to make some coffee."

"I'm sure she wasn't," laughed Tony, restraining an eager Liz with his hand. "Thank you, but I really must go. I ran into my brother on the way and he's waiting for me down the road. I said I wouldn't keep him waiting too long. But I promise to come round again. I've taken a great liking to you all, and Christopher will always be someone special to me. I shall make it in my way to try to see him as soon as possible. If you have any contact with him in the meantime, tell him that another prodigal returned home, thanks to him, humanly speaking. He'll know what I mean."

Liz also knew what he meant. "You became a christian!" she cried eagerly. "Christopher will consider everything worthwhile because of that."

Tony Masterson's face suddenly lost all dignity and became that of a little boy having been offered the chance of a ride beside the engine driver!

"I'm twenty years younger since that conversation with your brother, Elizabeth! I suppose every prodigal feels like that when he is welcomed home. It is the knowledge that you *are* welcome, in spite of what you've been and what you deserve. Christopher Meyer should train for the ministry," he said, then his face clouded. "There are many more people in the same state as I was. Not quite so many would hit the rocks if there was always a Christopher at hand. One day I'll tell you my story. However, I really must go now. Good night to you all. I won't forget, in the morning. By the way, here's my card."

As he walked out of the bright arc of light outside the front door, Tony Masterson became a waving silhouette and then he was lost in the darkness.

David ushered the little group back inside. As soon as the door was shut, Liz leaned on David's shoulder and burst into tears, surprisingly to his pleasure rather than embarrassment.

Paul choked back his laughter. "Women!" he exclaimed. "You'd think we'd had bad news. Come on, Alan, let's leave them to it."

They were too occupied in general rejoicing to hear Tony Masterson's footsteps die away and, shortly after, a car engine start up in the gloom of a garden hedge not far away. But when Liz and Alan returned home a quarter of an hour later, the car was nowhere to be seen.

Chapter 8

The next day their almost uncontrollable delight and relief turned back to bewilderment and sickness of heart when the expected notification of Christopher's imminent release did not come. Liz had even expected that he might be home before her! Instead, everything was just the same as usual, her mother quietly doing jobs around the house and her father busy on the weekend's messages in his study. They did not look up with subdued excitement to say that they had news. All of Liz's forebodings returned, all the stronger following the high hopes of the day, and she was glad she had subdued the impulse the night before to tell them everything. She would not have wanted them to share this feeling of floating in the air one minute, then painfully hitting the ground the next.

She could not understand the silence. She could hardly believe it. Tony Masterson had promised to

107

go to the police first thing that morning. Surely that allowed sufficient time for all the red tape to be well and truly cut! Could it be possible that the police had not believed him? She couldn't believe that Tony would not keep his word. He had given his promise and he would keep it for was he not a christian now? So why, *why* then this silence?

She pulled herself up with a start. She was expecting Tony to act like the christian he now was. Then so must she, who had been one for years. She was forgetting again that God had promised, 'In all thy ways acknowledge Him and He shall direct thy paths'.

To acknowledge Him was her constant aim, therefore He surely expected her to trust in His direction. Here she was acting as if the whole outcome depended upon her! As if He were not in control!

"Don't go out tonight, Liz," pleaded her mother. "You look tired."

So Alan went over to David's house on his own to see if any news had arrived there. In his turn, David was wondering why he had not heard anything from the manse. He could not hide his consternation when Alan explained that there was nothing to hear, for nothing had happened. All day long, David had never doubted that it was just a matter of time. So the silence was like a slap in the face.

"Perhaps the police didn't believe him," Paul suggested. "Or maybe he is ill or had an accident, so that he hasn't been able to go."

"Perhaps! Maybe! If! How? Why? When? How much longer are those going to be our favourite words?" David complained impatiently.

Alan soon returned home, feeling fit only for his own company. He and Christopher had always been very close and he was extremely disappointed at the turn of events. He could only hope that something had temporarily prevented Tony Masterson from going to the police. But even if he had become ill, as Paul suggested, he could no doubt have got in touch by telephone. Perhaps an accident was more likely.

Determinedly, Alan shook off his worry, and spent the journey back home in silent prayer that God would come to their help, that His will might be done and that they themselves would be kept in His will.

The following day was a repeat of the previous one. Liz and Alan endured yet another day which seemed a year in duration, then returned to an unchanged home. Liz could not sit around another evening so she set off for the Ransoms' house as soon as the tea things were cleared away. Alan reluctantly stayed at home, declaring that he had a month's homework to do in a night.

A sharp, wintry wind blew leaves across Liz's pathway and into her face. It was something to fight with and eased her tension and frustration. She arrived as David was walking away from the telephone.

"That was Dr. Mason," he told her. "He was

ringing to find out what is going on as he had expected to hear again before now. As if we know what is going on!''

"What did he say when you told him?"

"That we'd not to worry. Something had obviously happened to prevent Tony from keeping his promise at the moment but that he no doubt would as soon as he could. What I'd like to know is exactly what that thing is, short of a thunderbolt having hit his house, his being kidnapped, or a bomb in his car — which is supposed to be out of order, anyway — and this moment lying unconscious in hospital.''

David's tone was heavily sarcastic and Elizabeth found herself flying to Tony Masterson's defence.

"Stop, David!" she pleaded. "It might turn out to be true. Things like that *do* happen. But you don't believe any of them. You are merely being derisive. It's peculiar, I admit, but Tony won't let us down.''
Faced with David's doubt, she really believed that.

David's face did not alter. "Who wouldn't be derisive?" he asked. "I'm highly sceptical of any worthwhile outcome, in spite of Dr. Mason's reassuring words. We might as well have kept out of the whole thing for all the good we have done! I don't believe that man was Tony at all. He just came to con us.''

"David!" It was a cry of anguish.

"He didn't tell us anything," David went on mercilessly. "All he did was to agree with the things we put in the paper. Can you imagine that kind of a man being in trouble? He struck me as a person with himself very much in control. And if he were in trouble, can you imagine his turning to a young lad like Christopher for help? He was an educated, executive type . . . "

"And that type, as you call him, would have better things to do than answer an SOS advert as a lark," Liz retorted, her face flaming. "And he could be in trouble just like anyone else. Business ulcers and all that! Christopher's grown up, so why shouldn't he confide in him if Christopher had the answers he was seeking? The Gospel is effective for all classes of men, whether you admit it or not. I say Tony Masterson was genuine."

"Then why didn't he do what he said he would do?" David persisted pointedly. Then he recalled a comment of Dr. Mason's. "The doctor didn't agree with Tony that a gang was involved. He thought it was nonsense to suppose an amateur, intent on personal spite, would have placed a traceable valuable in Christopher's flat to incriminate him because, if a motive were there, it would betray himself. That sounds sense. Neither did he think an 'expert' crook would bungle it the way this was bungled. His advice was to wait until Tony clears this lot up."

"So *he* believes in Tony, then?"

David shrugged. "He's no reason not to. He didn't meet him. But I did and I'm not sure of him. As I said why didn't he keep his promise?"

Liz sighed, deflated again. "I don't know," she

admitted. "David, will you come to the police station with me?"

"If you believe Tony as much as you say, why don't you simply wait for him to do as he said?"

"Please, David."

"Sorry, Liz. Dr. Mason advised us not to. He said to be content to wait and to be satisfied with getting Christopher freed."

"I don't mean to tell them of our suspicions about . . . about you know whom. Only to find out whether Tony has been . . . There might be reasons for their not . . . "

Taking the address card Tony had given them out of his wallet, David strode through to the phone and dialled the number supplied. Liz wondered why she had not thought of that. But there was no reply. "Wait until I get my coat and shoes," David said resignedly, replacing the receiver.

"Oh, thanks, David. By the way, where's Paul?"

"He's got a cold. I sent him to bed with a hot water bottle. It's nothing, really, but I thought I'd better play safe. In actual fact, I suspect he's getting his paperwork up to date, rather than sleeping off his cold. He doesn't realise I know, but he keeps it under the mattress. His is a hundred per cent dedication, true detective fashion."

They smiled and Liz said, "He's a good lad, David. What did he think of Tony?"

"Quite impressed. I'll get my things."

Liz poked her head round Paul's door and talked to him until David was ready to go. There was no sign of book or pens when she went in but the light was on and he had had plenty of warning of her approach. She had only been there a few minutes when David called, but Paul had cheered her up somewhat with his nonsense chatter.

It was about a mile to the police station. In order both to save time and to keep warm, they decided to go by bus. There were few other passengers and there was no difficulty in getting a seat together. As soon as the bus set off, big drops of rain began to splatter on the windows and run down, leaving narrow runnels like teardrops down a dirty face.

"It is amazing how few people seem to have seen our advert," Liz said. "Mum and Dad obviously haven't. Only one other person has mentioned it to me. Which makes it all the more miraculous that the one person that mattered saw it." Her voice was firm. "Anyone mentioned it to you?"

"The same. One, that's all. A man at work. He knew the advert related to the Hampshire diamonds case, and naturally assumed that your father had put it in the paper. I gave as noncommittal an answer as I could."

"Let's get off the bus here, David. I think it will be nearer than the next stop."

A few minutes later, wet and cold, they were standing at a desk in a brightly lit room at the police headquarters. A man in uniform faced them impassively, no doubt longing for his supper. He looked at them more keenly when they had explained the nature of their enquiry.

"Sorry to disappoint you but no-one reported here, either in person or by phone."

They had known that this reply to their query was the most likely one but it came as a blow to hear it in so many words. Moved by their visible distress, the constable waited a moment or two then encouraged them to explain further.

"I recognise you as Christopher Meyer's sister," he smiled kindly at Elizabeth through his bushy eyebrows, "and I can understand your disappointment if you expected the missing man to have turned up. Perhaps you'd explain exactly what has happened to bring you here tonight."

They both began to speak at once.

"Miss Meyer," interrupted the policeman. "You have actually met a man who claims to be the missing Tony?"

"Yes. He called on us as a result of an advertisement we put in the newspaper."

"Did he tell you his surname?"

"Masterson."

"You know of his whereabouts?"

David held out the private card Tony had given them. "His address is on that," he said.

"And he admitted he was the same Tony your brother spoke to on the night of the robbery?"

"He did and he promised to come here the following morning — yesterday. I can't believe he didn't mean it." Liz cried brokenly.

"Yes, I see," the man facing them replied. "Not to worry, Miss Meyer. With this address," he tapped the card with a pencil, "we can soon check up on him."

"But don't you see what it means?" Liz argued. "Something must have happened to stop him coming. I'm sure he would have come if he could. Perhaps he's in hospital . . . ?"

The constable reached across the desk for the telephone. They realized he was going to contact the local hospital. It was some time before the reply came and when it did it was in the negative.

"You gathered what the answer was? They have no patient at the hospital of that name. Leave it with me, now. We'll contact Mr. Masterson and get in touch with you again. Perhaps you'd let me have your name and address," he said, supplying David with pen and paper. While David was writing he went on, "I hope for your sakes that I can report a happy outcome when I contact you again. Were your parents present when this man called on you, Miss Meyer?"

Liz explained yet again the absence of her parents at that meeting with Tony Masterson.

"I've no criticism of your motive," he replied when she'd finished, "but you would have been wiser not to have worked quite so much on your own. So there were only the two of you present to meet the man?"

"We both have brothers. They were present," David replied. "Aged thirteen and fifteen," he added reluctantly, anticipating the question.

Their interrogator half smiled. "You did well to

get your man, anyway," he said. "What was he like? Can you describe him?"

"Distinguished. Prematurely grey," David said, seeing Tony Masterson clearly in his mind. "He was small and very well spoken."

"Hmm. Well, we'll find him if he is to be found."

"He *is* . . . " Liz began impatiently but broke off when David nudged her. "Thanks." She swallowed hard. "I guess it has got beyond us."

"Don't worry," the constable said again. "We'll do all we can."

There seemed to be nothing more to say, so Liz and David went back out into the cold, making their way home on foot, for they would be home by the time the next bus was due.

"Liz," David said suddenly with determination of his face as they struggled against the wind and rain. "I think we have to face the facts. That policeman didn't know whether to believe us, in spite of his reassurances, and I'm not at all sure that I believe the man who claims to be Christopher's Tony. In fact, I'm pretty sure he's not the person we are looking for. If that is so, we are no nearer than when we started. Dr. Mason was right, that advert *was* a long shot — too long."

"Why do you say that?" the girl demanded. "Just because we've had another setback and don't know all the answers yet!" She put her chin in the air but soon put it down again as the dust blew up her nose. "At least give the police a chance to follow up our lead. I don't know why you are so determined

116

not to trust Tony Masterson."

"I explained before. Besides, he overdid the part. He was *too* convincing, if you know what I mean."

"No, I don't," Liz replied emphatically. "How can anyone be too convincing? You are turning into a mystic, David."

David sighed at the stubbornness in her voice. Oh, well! He hadn't expected her to listen. It was no use arguing once she had made up her mind.

They continued as fast as they could in the direction of home. By this time it was raining very heavily, its penetrating coldness beginning to make itself felt through their clothes. The driving rain stung their faces and they walked with their heads so low that they almost walked into the car standing outside the gates of the manse. The driver was just preparing to get out. When he saw the two figures approaching, he shut the door again and opened the window beside the driving seat.

"I say, is that Elizabeth?"

The girl whirled round and stared into the car. "Who is it?" she asked doubtfully.

"John — John Barrett. I was round this way and thought I would call."

David stared hard to see this cousin of Christopher's but it was too dark to see anything but his outline.

"Oh, er . . . hello. Come on then. We're just going in."

"Actually, I should be getting back, if you don't mind. I'm later than I expected, so I'll call another time. Remember me to your folks though, won't you? It is difficult fitting everything in just now — wedding details and so on, you know." He looked keenly at David standing close beside his cousin, but Liz did not satisfy his curiosity. "I . . . er . . . saw the advert in the paper and I thought — that is — I wondered if you'd had any reply. Naturally, it would be a great relief to you — all the family — if the missing man came forward."

Liz spoke in the sweetest of tones. "John, I'm sorry. We're wet through already and my teeth are chattering, so we can't stay to talk, I'm afraid. We'll let you know when there's anything definite, don't worry. All we can say at the moment is that we have a lead that should take us to him. If you really won't come in, we'll have to say goodnight."

"That should keep him guessing," Liz said as they squelched up the wet path to the kitchen door. "Come in, David, and get a warm up before you go on."

"Not tonight. I'll get home and into some dry clothes. There's no point in having to warm up twice. That was an interesting episode with your cousin. He obviously wanted to know. He'll not want to lose his house now, if they've started on the decorating! But we'll talk about it tomorrow. Be seeing you, Liz."

Chapter 9

On Friday lunch time, David and Liz met once more in the town centre. It was Liz's birthday and her parents had given her money to buy a new camera. Though she felt to have little heart for buying anything at present, she had the sense to see that she must make the effort for her parents' sake, and there was a particular one she had had her eye on for a while. So, having the money in her purse, she led David straight towards the shop where she had seen the coveted model. However, knowing that she was going to buy a camera, they looked as a matter of interest in other photography shop windows which served only to give Liz doubts as to whether she was choosing the right one. Consequently, they decided to shop around for a while, comparing models and prices.

It was while they were thus engaged that David suddenly spotted the ummistakable figure of Tony

Masterson crossing the road ahead. The small, grey haired figure had not seen them.

"Come on," David cried eagerly, grabbing his companion's arm, and pulled her unceremoniously along after him.

Liz opened her mouth to object to such rough, ungentlemanly handling, then saw Tony for herself.

Seeing them rushing towards him, the man glanced curiously at them then looked away again.

"Surely he recognises us," David muttered.

"People look different in different situations," Liz gasped, panting for breath. "Tony! Tony! Mr. Masterson!"

The man stopped dead in his tracks but looked as if he might have tried to shake off the hand that Liz instinctively extended to his arm. A flicker of wariness mingled with the surprise on his face.

"Oh, hello there," he said politely, but David thought it sounded more like a question than a greeting. Liz did not seem to notice.

"Oh, Mr. Masterson, how glad we are to see you! We've been wondering whatever had happened. When you never went to the police we thought you must have had an accident, or something."

Tony's face relaxed somewhat. "Well, you can see I'm alright," he replied a little hesitantly.

David sensed that the man was thinking fast behind the cover of slow speech. Suddenly he was furiously angry with him for what he took as evasiveness and the feigned inability to recognise them at first.

"Some people's word is as uncertain as the weather," he snapped coldly. "You gave us your promise that you would report to the police the morning after we met you. That was three days ago. What kept you?" His tone was very sarcastic.

"Oh, David, don't be so angry," Liz scolded and turned pleadingly to the older man. "Mr. Masterson, it's just that we are so anxious for Christopher to . . . to be freed. You no doubt have good reasons for not keeping your promise, but you *will* go to the police, won't you?"

The man's demeanour softened and he patted her hand. "Don't you worry," he said, "I'll go this very afternoon. In a few minutes, in fact. Really, I do owe you an apology. Actually, I've been in a spot of difficulty the last few days. I can't explain very well here and now but, believe me, I would have gone if I could. Now, if you will excuse me, I have an urgent business appointment. After that — I won't forget. Nice to see you again."

With a brief salute he left them alone again before they had time to object. They hesitated, standing staring at each other in the middle of the pavement. Gradually becoming conscious of being in the way of passers by, they moved slowly away without a word, too unsure of their own reactions for the moment to make any comment. The whole affair became more bewildering with every new event. Liz shivered and suddenly became capable of speech.

"David, I'm sorry, there *is* something strange about Tony Masterson. I don't know how you detected it the other evening, but I can see it today. He seemed so different, somehow."

"I could have hit him," David growled aggressively.

"So I noticed," Liz giggled, cheering up. "Never mind. If he keeps his promise this time I'll forgive him for acting almost as if he didn't know us. He did imply there had been reasons for his silence before. We've got to trust him, David but . . . but . . . oh, I'm so disappointed in him, all the same."

"There's no reason to feel disappointed if he keeps his word."

"But there is! Disappointment in him rather than in what he has or has not done. When we first met him he seemed so concerned and open . . . and . . ."

"And completely in control of the situation," David continued for her, "whereas today he was uncertain, because we caught him unawares."

"You still don't trust him, do you?"

David shrugged. "I'd say he was a worried man, for some reason."

"Never mind. The police will sort him out. They mustn't have got round to checking up on him. Save them the trouble if he goes himself. Now come on. Which camera are you going to decide on?"

Liz glanced at her watch. "I think I'll stick to the original one," she said with an apologetic grin, "but there isn't time now. We'd better go and eat. The camera will do tomorrow if we're coming to town as usual."

David nodded and they strode off in the direction of a little cafe where they often ate or simply enjoyed a cup of the excellent coffee. Today they decided to add cream cakes in honour of Liz's birthday.

"I told Mum and Dad about the advertisement last night, David," Liz informed him as they walked side by side.

"Did they put a curse on me for encouraging you?"

"Don't be stupid, David. You know they are not like that. More likely they were glad of your restraining influences over me! I had to tell them because of the police ringing up. They agreed there had been nothing to lose by it and were rather impressed by our initiative, I think." She chuckled. "Though Dad did ask if it was my idea, like most of the mad schemes in our household. I could honestly say that it wasn't entirely mine, in this case."

"Did you discuss any of the other aspects with them?"

"I mentioned the Lester Addison episode in the cafe, in a casual sort of way. But not John Barrett. My nerve failed me there," she admitted. "Anyway, they were only ideas, after all, and we've no proof that either of them are involved. They certainly have a motive and we've actually seen Lester acting suspiciously, but I'm taking Dr. Mason's advice and forgetting that aspect. I simply want Christopher cleared. I did tell them John had been round enquiring though."

"Did you tell them about Dr. Mason's help?"

"Yes. They thought it had been a wise move," she answered slowly, "but I suspected Dad would have liked us to have consulted them instead — though they understood why we hadn't. Mum said she knew we had something on our minds, but hadn't guessed we were doing some private sleuthing!" She glanced sideways at David and added, "Dad said we had to be careful not to try to force God's hand and try to do His work for Him."

"We've been given minds to use ourselves," David argued with a stubborn glint in his eyes.

"Yes, but our minds are fallible and as subject to error as are our bodies. They both need to be subject to Him."

"Thanks for the sermon," David laughed. "Now let's get some food for our bodies. We're here," and he held the cafe door open for her. "It will have to be a snack but we should survive until teatime. However, you shall have the promised cream cake, birthday girl!"

"I wonder if there will be any news when we get home," Liz pondered with a slight shiver.

"Oh, I expect so," David replied comfortingly. "The police don't stand on ceremony."

The news waiting for Liz and Alan at home was not good.

"The police have been round to the address you gave them several times," Mrs. Meyer told them wearily. "No-one answered until their last visit, when Mr. Masterson came to the door. He confirmed that he was Tony Masterson but, when they questioned him about Christopher Meyer and the contact he had made with you, he denied everything. He . . . "

"Oh, Mum, he couldn't!" Liz cried from the heart. "Why, we even saw him this lunch time when he promised again to go to the station. I can't believe it!"

Alan open mouthed with shock apparently couldn't believe it, either.

"Everything and everybody is going mad!" Liz stormed, then repeated, "I can't believe it! I keep thinking — and hoping — there can't be any more disappointments."

She caught her father's eyes, challenging but affectionate, and she raised her chin. "Though He slay me, yet will I trust in Him," she quoted defiantly, and they smiled at each other in complete understanding.

"Did the police believe him?" Alan interrupted thoughtfully.

"Difficult to say," Pastor Meyer replied, "but they can't do much without a statement from him."

"They knew that we had a private card with Tony's name and address on it, Alan pointed out. "How would we have got that unless he had given it to us?"

"That's a point, although a rather slender one, and I'll take it up with them — though they have no doubt thought of it," his father promised. "Now, though you are naturally disappointed, remember that your trust should never have been in what you were doing, nor even in your praying, but in the One Who answers prayer. I'm not saying it *was* misplaced — just reminding you. Right?"

Feeling surprisingly better, they ate their meal cheerfully and with a good appetite.

They gave David time to get home then rang him with the news.

"I could wring his neck!" David exploded indignantly, his voice so loud that Liz held the ear-phone away from her head, and she could not help smiling at his vehemence. "He's nothing but a phoney, a hypocrite and a liar!"

"I can't understand it," Liz admitted.

"It's clear enough," David retorted. "He's obviously not the right Tony, and he's leading us on for a lark. There are jokers like that, but I don't think much of their sense of humour. Sorry, Liz, not a very nice birthday present. Incidentally, Mum and Dad are coming home earlier than they intended and will be arriving in about an hour, so I'll not be round tonight. If you don't come here, we'll see you in the morning at the usual time. I'm sorry," he said again.

Saturday morning was their one regular meeting time. It was quite unusual for them to see each other every night as they had this week. On Saturdays they all went into town, Liz to shop for her mother, David to browse in the library and book shops and

126

Alan and Paul to spend their pocket money. Usually they ended up at their favourite little cafe.

But Liz had something to do which would not wait until the next day, when she had a free evening on her hands.

"Alan," she called up to her brother's room. "Have you finished your homework?"

"I've done all that my wayward mind will put an answer to," he called back somewhat ruefully. "I don't think there is any point in staring at it any longer. Why?"

She went up the stairs and spoke more quietly. "I feel like a cycle run."

"Oh?" he replied suspiciously. "In the balmy summer air, I suppose. Where to?'"

Her brother knew her well.

"Across town."

"Tony Masterson's?"

"Right first time. Are you coming?"

Alan looked at her doubtfully. "What's the point?" he asked resignedly. "I can't see that anything we might say would make him talk. Is David going?"

"He can't." She explained. "Come on. Please."

"I don't know whether we ought to."

"I shall still go if you don't."

"It's a bit like forcing God's hand . . . "

They argued a while, but eventually set off together on their bicycles. Liz felt a little guilty for dragging Alan out against his better judgement and for not informing anyone where they were going.

She ought to have left a note but it was too late when she thought of it.

"I presume you know exactly where we are going," Alan called over his shoulder as they sped along roads which were unusually quiet at this time of day.

"It's on Lancelot Road, number 24," she called back. "Don't go so fast, Alan. I can hardly keep up with you. I recall the address well enough, for I made a special point of memorising it before that policeman took the card with it on. Couldn't remember the phone number, though."

They stopped at the traffic lights, then pedalled on abreast.

"You'll have to do the talking," Alan told his sister.

"Don't I always? That's alright. I wouldn't be able to keep quiet, anyway!"

Nevertheless, Liz was rather worried. She didn't know what awaited them. Most likely there would be a wife who might, or might not, know the background to their visit, but the thought of Tony himself made her feel most apprehensive.

There was a garage still open with lights blazing at the road junction in front of them.

"We turn right here," Liz told Alan in good time for him to indicate. "We are nearly there."

She knew the district only slightly and they had to watch the street names to find Lancelot Road as all the streets looked alike, their pavements regimented with stubby, pollarded trees, behind which

128

impersonal privet hedges screened relatively new semi-detached bungalows.

"I'd turn into the wrong house sometimes if I lived here," Liz observed. "They are all so alike."

"This is number 10," Alan said, pointing. "So we must have begun at the lower numbers."

Number 24 looked exactly like the rest. There was a light behind one window and a car outside the garage.

Brother and sister leaned their bicycles against the hedge and walked towards the front door. Liz gave a bold ring at the bell before they had time to change their minds.

"There's someone coming," Alan murmured and Liz nodded. No-one came. They waited a moment longer then rang again. The sound of the bell vibrated through the house, then silence settled all around them.

"That's funny," Alan whispered. "I'm sure I heard movements inside."

"I thought so too. Perhaps we were mistaken."

"There's the car. And there's a light burning. Let's try the back."

It was very dark at the other side of the house and they had to grope their way close to the wall. There was no bell, so they knocked hard at the door. They grimaced at the loud noise it made in the quiet night air. All the same, when there was still no reply, they knocked again. Immediately, behind them an angry voice called from the next house.

"Are you trying to wake all the children?" it

demanded. "Can't you tell he must be out? If he'd been in, he'd have heard your first performance! And there is a bell at the front!"

"Oh, I'm sorry," Liz called back, "but we were sure someone was in because . . . " but the irate neighbour had gone. "Come on, Alan," she sighed, deflated. "If there is anyone at home, they obviously don't intend to come. As she said, they must have heard."

They groped back the way they had come and down the drive past the stationary car to the road.

As they moved away from the house, the curtain in one of the darkened windows moved slightly and an eye watched their departure. Then the curtain dropped once more into place.

Chapter 10

The events of Saturday morning began ordinarily enough. Alan and Liz got up, collected Mrs. Meyer's shopping list and set off at the usual time. Their house was further from the town than the Ransoms', so they called for David and Paul en route. Their friends were just setting off. As they joined each other at the gate, Mrs. Ransom called to them from the kitchen doorway.

"Post this letter for me, will you, please?" Paul ran back to collect the envelope in her hand. "It is to your Gran. She might as well have it now that I've written it, even though it isn't urgent." She watched Paul stuff it in his pocket. "Now, don't forget it, or get it all messed up with chocolate!"

Paul grinned because he knew that she was laughing at him.

"Have you got the money for your camera, Liz?" David asked later.

"Don't worry, she assured him. "It isn't every day I get the opportunity of buying 'big', so I couldn't possibly forget!"

Changing the subject, she told him and Paul about the previous evening. Paul hung on to every word.

David shook his head. "You're mad!" he cried hotly when she had finished. "It is perhaps just as well no-one came. Alan had more sense, trying to dissuade you from going. Anything might have happened."

Paul wondered why David was getting so hot around the collar, when it was quite clear that nothing had happened.

The shopping centre was crowded, and prolonged conversations therefore difficult. The swarming mass of humanity in the pedestrian precinct felt in danger of becoming solid.

"Anyone would think Christmas was coming," Paul grumbled. "It's like wading up to your neck in the sea — you are held back all the time."

"Don't worry, Junior," David consoled him. "By the time you get your comic, you'll not notice anything else. It will be everyone else worrying then, with you bumping into them."

Paul pulled a face at him and promptly walked into a hurrying figure coming the other way. David grabbed him by the scruff of the neck and hauled him along beside him, with Paul complaining loudly that he was not a dog.

Paul's comic was purchased first, but he was

given strict instructions to keep it in his pocket until he got home! Reluctantly, the boy complied. Putting it in his pocket, he felt the letter his mother had given him. He must not forget to post it.

Next, they shopped around for Mrs. Meyer's requirements, comparing prices at the various supermarkets. Liz enjoyed getting as much as she could for her money even when it wasn't her own money she was spending. For one thing, she knew that her mother liked to give all she could to the various christian missions and charities. Even though there were four of them, they soon had enough to carry. Liz was savouring to the full the pleasant anticipation of going for her camera, and now they were actually on their way for it.

"Dr. Mason has a beauty," Alan told them. "I once went to visit him with Dad and he showed it to us for some reason."

"Oh, that reminds me," David said. "He rang up again last night to find out what was happening."

"Nothing," Paul and Alan chorused bleakly.

"He seemed as mystified as we are," David went on. "When I suggested our theory that this chap was in it for a lark, he thought we might be right. If that were so, he thought the right Tony could still turn up. He said people don't always read papers as soon as they are out — they get passed on, and things like that — so his advice was to keep hoping."

"Yes, that's possible," Liz agreed, visibly brighter." All sorts of things catch my eye when I'm

133

lighting the fire." She stopped when Paul suddenly exclaimed and went pink in the face. "Whatever is the matter, Paul?"

Paul was too agitated to get any words out. They grabbed him as he stumbled, thinking he must be ill. Still mute, he pointed ahead and his companion spotted a grey haired man who had stopped to fasten a shoelace ahead of them. Tony Masterson's face was half turned in their direction. He straightened up as they watched and seemed to look directly at them through the gap between hurrying shoppers. In a sudden rush he picked up the suitcase on the pavement beside him and deliberately hurried away to join the thickest of the crowd. Instinctively, the four dashed after him, not knowing what they were going to do, but determined not to let him get away from them, as he was obviously intent on doing.

"Quick!" Liz cried desperately. "Don't let him get out of sight," and she sped on, weaving her way round people, prams, trolleys and lamp-posts. The other three unhappily got delayed behind a gang of high spirited youths who were monopolising the pavement, and they edged this way and that to get in front of them, losing a lot of time in the process. They were also carrying a lot more shopping than Liz.

The man turned round again, spotted Liz and rushed on, heedless of whom he knocked and pushed with his elbows and his suitcase. The more he tried to escape them, the angrier Liz became. She did not bother to wait for the boys, for fear of losing him. At the first opportunity she crossed over the road to the opposite pavement and was pleased to notice that her sudden idea had succeeded. Mr. Masterson had slowed down when he could no longer see her behind him. Trying to keep herself as concealed as possible behind groups of people, she now found it easier to follow.

David, Paul and Alan were still together, but they had lost sight of both Tony Masterson and Liz. David was worried about Liz in case she found herself in trouble. She was so inclined to act first and only think afterwards. He groaned aloud. If only they could return to their former uneventful existences! He put out both hands, stopping the two boys in their tracks.

"It's no use going on," he said. "We don't know which way they have gone. Liz will want to find us again — eventually! — so I suggest we go back to the point where we set off after that fellow and wait for her there. Otherwise, we'll never meet again. She'll probably realise we'll do that."

They had no ideas so together they retraced their steps and waited, expecting Liz to return before long. They held on to their shopping bags to start with, but put them down against a shop window when the weight began to pull on their arms. Paul, considering it a legitimate excuse, pulled out his comic and began to read. David paced up and down to relieve his agitation, while Alan stood with his back to the window and scanned the distance for the first glimpse of his sister. It was enough having one member of the family in trouble.

"Paul," he broke in on his friend's diversions. "What do you think?" David was still pacing a distance away.

"Lots of things," came Paul's prompt reply. "The trouble is that they don't fit together. A whole lot of contradictions aren't easy to build up into a story."

"You've no idea as to what really happened?"

"Not even as to Chapter one!" Paul groaned. "I think we have quite a few significant facts in our possession, and I've come up with a few theories. I think the John Barrett and Lester Addison aspect needs looking further into. I also think we haven't attached enough importance to several apparently insignificant details — such as that stationary car on Monday and Tuesday night. I think that Tony Masterson could tell us something if he would, but I also think . . . I *know* . . . I'm beaten!"

Alan nodded dejectedly. "I thought everything was going to be alright the first time we met Mr. Masterson. Somehow, the man we talked to then is completely separate in my mind from the man we've seen today. He . . . "

"He's a clever actor or a loony, that's all." David had paced back to them and overheard the last part of the sentence.

"You mean he's not the man Christopher helped at all?"

"I haven't the faintest idea what I mean, Paul! This lot's beyond me and I refuse to try to work it

136

out any longer."

"But if he's not the Tony Christopher met, why bother claiming to be?" Alan objected. "After all, he's done nothing but try to avoid us ever since!"

"Most likely it was meant as a joke. Some people have a warped sense of humour," David replied. "Unfortunately for him, the joke got out of hand, for he didn't count on running into us again."

"That can't be right, Big Brother," Paul contradicted emphatically, "For he himself gave us his name and address."

David sighed impatiently. He looked at his watch. It was time Liz was coming back. She had been away for nearly twenty minutes. He didn't like it. He stared absently into the shop window behind them but he didn't really see the toys, games and fireworks on display there. He was contemplating small, feminine Liz thinking she could take on the case of the Hampshire diamonds on her brother's behalf unaided — or at least with only their uncertain help. They had been very naive to think they could turn a single stone.

Paul went back to his comic but he wasn't reading it any longer. He was juggling in his mind with facts and suppositions and probabilities. He, too, was thinking of Liz and wishing they hadn't got separated from her.

They waited until half an hour had passed, by which time they were beginning to feel chilly around fingers and toes.

"Perhaps Liz expected us to go to the photographic shop, seeing that is where we were going anyway."

"Right," David replied, seizing it as a probable explanation and hoping it was the right one. "You go along there, Alan. It's not far and, if she's there, you might as well get the camera then both of you return here. We'd better stay, just in case."

Alan, glad of any action, was quick to comply. The others watched him disappear through a nearby arcade. But the fair haired boy was soon back on his own. They did not need to see the shrug of his shoulders or the shake of his head to tell them she hadn't been there, for his crestfallen face told them. He rejoined them silently and they continued to stand there getting more and more worried by the minute. Fantastic visions of Liz attacked or kidnapped stole unbidden into their minds.

"Three quarters of an hour," David muttered.

No sooner had he said it than the girl appeared suddenly in view again. She was running as quickly as the crowds would allow and peering ahead to see if they were there. She waved in her relief when she saw them. Her relief was no greater than that of the boys, who suddenly felt strangely like waving flags and singing. Liz, however, did not give them time for such niceties, for she had plenty to say. After pausing only long enough to get sufficient breath to speak, she gave them a graphic account of the events they had missed.

"Quick!" she gasped, hardly able to contain herself. "There's no time to lose! We've got to do something! Listen carefully," She took another few quick gasps of air and clutched at her side.

"Get your breath back and calm down."

"No time," she retorted, then repeated, "Listen. When it became obvious that Tony Masterson was intent on escaping from us, I was so mad I was determined he wouldn't! I didn't think out what I was doing. I felt so outraged against the way he was treating us and — and Christopher — that from that moment automatic reactions seemed to make me do the right things and take me to the right place at the right time."

"Tony was heading for the station. By then he obviously thought he had shaken me off. He went on to platform five. I chose platform four. As you know, there is a waiting room between those two platforms with doors on to both. Through the windows between us I could just see his left shoulder and the rest of him was hidden by the wall, so I felt it was safe to go into the waiting room. He might not have spotted me had he looked in for it was crowded, but I was careful, all the same. Just as I reached a position where there was only the one sheet of glass between his shoulder and myself, a man went up to him. You'll never guess who!" but she did not give them time to guess. "It was that dark man with a moustache we saw talking to Lester Addison in the cafe — remember, David? It was clear they knew each other. I couldn't tell what they said at first, for there was too much noise in the room behind me. But there was a 'Ladies' to my right, so I went in and grabbed the first cubicle, where there was a small, high, frosted window partly open. I'm afraid I stood on the seat, but I don't think British Rail would mind if they knew what a good cause it was in and, what's more, I could hear perfectly there. Tony was telling 'Moustache' — for want of a better name — that the boss, (he referred to someone as Boss in the cafe, didn't he, David?) the boss had instructed him to go to a place I'd never heard of and can't remember now, so that he would not get to Crow End before evening. If Moustache was going there straight-away, he might as well take the letter for Joe that the boss had given him. Moustache said he'd come to the station to get the train times and that he had three quarters of an hour to get a meal before the next train. He was going straight to Crow End and might as well take the letter."

Liz looked at them keenly to make sure she had the whole of their attention. She need not have worried. "Now hold on to each other for this part and you'll know why I'm worked up! Tony Masterson then told Moustache that the boss had promised dire consequences if that letter should go astray because, not only did it give details of the next job, but also took the lid off the Hampshire and Gallery affairs, if it got into the wrong hands! Joe was to read it, then burn it immediately. He then said he would be glad to get rid of it as *those kids were after him!* I leaned so far towards the opening of the window that I nearly slipped but I did manage to see a blue envelope exchange hands. Moustache placed it carefully in the front part of his briefcase. They separated and Moustache went into the railway buffet." She pointed a finger at them. "Don't you see, when he mentioned the Hampshire affair, he must have meant the Hampshire diamonds and the Gallery affair was a theft of paintings, if you remember."

"Why didn't you ring the police from the platform?" David demanded, amazement all over his face.

"I tried to," Liz replied. "Believe it or not, every station phone was engaged and had a queue outside. I even attempted to jump the queues saying it was dreadfully urgent, but everyone insisted that their business was urgent, too, and stood their ground. The Police Station is a good quarter of an hour's walk away, so I hadn't time to go there and expect them to be able to catch him."

David frowned. "So?" he asked pointedly. "What now?"

Liz looked him defiantly in the eye. "We follow him until we manage to get that letter."

"Elizabeth Meyer! Are you going out of your senses? He's going on a train in . . . in about ten minutes from now."

"Then we shall go on a train in about ten minutes from now! We *must* get that letter!" she cried through clenched teeth.

"And how do we do that? Twist his arm in the middle of a crowded train?" David was desperate now to weaken Liz's mad resolve. "We don't know where he is going — it could be the north of Scotland for all we know — and we've no means of letting anyone know anything. How do we get a letter out of someone else's briefcase without anyone noticing and have you forgotten that these characters are obviously experienced criminals and not careless amateurs?"

"I don't know how anything! I just want that letter! Perhaps he'll go to sleep and give us our chance. After all, he won't be on his guard because he won't know us. And he can't be going to the north of Scotland, for the one train that sets off at that time only does a two hour journey. Come on, we are wasting time arguing!"

"Only! A mere afternoon pleasure trip, I must say!"

Liz started moving impatiently away from him in the direction of the station. David followed reluctantly, suspecting tears in her eyes but still arguing fiercely, while Paul and Alan with exchanged glances silently made up the rear.

"What about all this shopping and the little matter of money for fares?"

"We go past your office," she called over her shoulder, "and can leave the bags there. And have you forgotten my camera money?"

Somehow, arguing all the time, they reached the station before the train in question was due to leave. David and Elizabeth were nearer to falling out than they had ever been.

"*Please*, David! You haven't any other suggestion without losing Moustache and that letter. I promise we'll phone someone — the police, home — as soon as we can. See! The train is in — and Moustache is getting into that non-smoker."

Without another word she dashed into the booking office and asked for tickets. David was very angry, mainly because he was at a complete loss as to what he should do and allow the others to do. The situation was rapidly turning into a nightmare for him.

Alan and Paul had done little but listen in subdued excitement. They were all in favour of a train journey and keeping the briefcase containing the all important letter in sight. No harm could surely come to them in the middle of a trainful of people.

The guard was shutting the doors. Liz dashed up with their tickets, gave the boys a challenging glare and leaped on to the train. As she disappeared into the same non-smoker compartment as Moustache, the other three were galvanised into action and sprang after her. The door clanged noisily after them, the whistle blew and the train began to move.

Chapter 11

Liz went straight to the part of the compartment where Moustache had seated himself. There were three vacant seats around the table behind which he sat. Smiling sweetly, she enquired whether they were anyone's seats.

"Not at all. I don't mind a pretty girl to look at. Help yourself," Moustache told her.

Liz immediately took a dislike to him but she nevertheless thanked him just as her companions reached her. David motioned Alan to take the seat next to her, while he led Paul two tables down the compartment. Liz gathered that it was David's way of showing his displeasure with her and her mad escapades. The all important briefcase was safely on the rack above Moustache's head. The seats opposite were occupied by a party of curious middle aged ladies who appeared to be intent on noticing everything there was to notice about their fellow passengers. Liz hoped they would get off at the next station and that Moustache wouldn't. Moustache didn't, but neither did the ladies! Liz and Alan made a pretence of doing the crossword puzzle in a newspaper which had been left on their seat but in a rather half-hearted fashion for their minds were elsewhere all the time — in actual fact, in the briefcase only a few feet away from them, where there was a priceless piece of paper able to clear Christopher once and for all of the guilt of a crime he had never committed in the first place.

Moustache stared out of the window at a dull, unchanging landscape, he idly watched the two young people opposite him, he took a railway timetable from his pocket and read it, he did several other things, but not once did he look remotely like going to sleep. And even if he had, those inquisitive eyes opposite would have known straight away that the briefcase was his and not theirs. Liz had to make a great effort to keep her eyes off it, for its presence seemed to draw them. When she thought about what was in it, she felt that it rightly belonged to her because it would give to her brother what was rightly his, his freedom and innocence. If it took the 'lid off the Hampshire affair', and the other one too, then it would be in the course of justice to take it and unmask the wicked brains behind it. She was most concerned about the one aspect involving Christopher, though. She would gladly have paid more than her camera money if she could have extracted that one item. In fact, she felt she would have given every penny she possessed. For one moment she looked at Moustache wondering if he would sell, then she realised wryly that all she possessed would be like chicken feed to diamond thieves! Unobtrusively, she committed the matter again to her heavenly Father, Who was just as much in that train beside them as Moustache was, and then told herself to stop worrying. How she did insist on doing God's work for Him!

The rhythm of the axles made her feel sleepy, but apparently not Moustache nor the inquisitive ladies. Once, the dark man got up and Liz willed him to walk away down the train, but all he did was to remove his jacket and place it on the rack with his briefcase.

Liz felt sick with apprehension. They were getting on with their journey and were no nearer their objective. She wished that those nattering women would not stare. She tried staring back, but they merely smiled benignly at her and she could not help but smile, too. Perhaps if she had the chance to get that letter they could be made to understand. Maybe their curiosity would be satisfied on encountering a real life drama going on right beside them!

Alan had stopped trying to talk to her and, in spite of his intention, was nodding. Liz could see the top of David's head two seats away and she could well imagine his agitation as he waited for anything to happen. Poor David was too cautious to choose escapades like this. But he *had* come and not

146

abandoned her completely, even if against his better judgement.

The train came out of a tunnel and approached another station.

Liz had never been on this line before. So far there had been little to gaze out at, even if she'd felt like it. One town had merged into another. Trains always saw the back of things, she pondered, regarding the piled dumps behind warehouses, the untidy November vegetable gardens of the estates and the rusty, abandoned vehicles behind garages. Then the vista became less industrial, the buildings became sparser and fields increased in number. Villages became the norm. The train did not stop at many of them. They had been travelling for an hour and a half. In that time there had been a lot of changes in their compartment, passengers getting out and others replacing them, but Moustache and the ladies remained. Liz was a good talker, but she felt sure that the ladies would win a prize against her any day. Moustache, on the other hand, had not spoken a word since his 'pretty girl" remark, nor taken any interest in his surroundings.

The train was slowing again, and a rather dreary station misnamed Blossom Bridge appeared along-side. Without warning and without a glance at anyone, Moustache got up, donned his coat, grabbed his briefcase and joined a handful of other people at the carriage door. Liz did not move until the man was off and striding away towards the station exit. Then, removing the restraining hand she had placed on Alan's arm, she too prepared for a hurried exit. David and Paul did not need nudging, but followed meekly off the train. Either David had become resigned to her madness, Liz told herself amusedly, or else now the man had gone, he was simply visualising their sitting on the station platform waiting for a return train. But Liz had got her teeth in and she was not likely to let go if she could help it.

The train's diesel engine started up like a bus on rails and it slid away round a curve in the track and was lost to sight under a bridge, leaving them standing there unresolved and lost. Only now did they look around them. It was an unmanned station, its buildings empty and decrepit. There was no telephone, so they could not let anyone know where they were. There was no sign even of a village outside.

Moustache had left the platform and they cautiously followed. In the station yard, to their dismay, they saw him, complete with the precious briefcase, get into the passenger seat of a large blue car and drive away. Liz was vexed and half looked round for a taxi with the thought of dramatically getting it to tail the blue car, but she knew all the time that there would not be one. The only other car in sight was a battered estate car obviously there to meet one of the other passengers from the train.

The driver of this other car was watching them standing irresolutely there and he called over.

"Everything alright? Are you waiting for someone?"

"We are a bit lost, actually," Liz called back, seizing her chance. "We have come a long way and don't know the district. No-one is coming for us and we are wanting to find a place called 'Crow End'."

Liz heard David's stifled gasp and realised that her second supposition had been the correct one — he was imagining the next thing on the agenda to be the return journey.

"Crow End? That's alright. I'll give you a lift. Plenty of room, if not first class. I'm going right past the place."

Glad that they had discarded all their bags and baggage temporarily at David's office, they all piled into the vehicle, not without strong objection from David, but Liz ignored him. There was still a look of determination on her face and David sighed and shut up. If they did not end up today in trouble either from the crooks or the police he would be very surprised, but his sensible opinions obviously counted for nothing with Liz in this mood.

They travelled the narrow, winding, high-walled lanes at breakneck speed, and the driver talked as fast as he drove. Isolated trees and houses went past in a blur. Liz wondered what would happen if they met another vehicle, but the picture was so vivid that she stopped wondering. The woman beside the driver who had also got off the train evidenced no alarm. Alan and Paul were together in the back and every time the vehicle lurched round a corner one of them landed on top of the other. Alan grinned at one point, handing back the comic which had flown out of Paul's pocket at one such collision. Again Paul was reminded of his mother's letter.

"Alan, me boy," he groaned. "All that trailing round and all that standing waiting for Liz, and I forgot to post Mum's letter! I'll be for it!"

"You'll be for it for more than one thing, after today!" Alan prophesied dolefully under cover of the driver's ceaseless chatter at the front, "and so will we. Mum and Dad are pretty understanding, but this is going to take some explaining."

Paul nodded. Their respective families would even now be wondering where they had got to, and they were miles from home and without plans for getting back there. Most of their combined resources had been used for the train fares, so there was no booking a night's lodgings if there was no getting back today. He smiled to himself, visualising them all creeping on to a comfortable bed of hay in one of the many barns there seemed to be in this area. However, there was still plenty of that day left. It had been less than a two hour journey, so they weren't stranded yet. His greatest concern was on account of the worry they would cause at home unless they managed to get a message there before long.

The car suddenly screeched to a halt, making them all grab for something to steady themselves.

The driver laughed. "I'm used to these roads," he boasted. "I could drive round them blindfolded and this old bus knows them on its own. Out with you if you want Crow End. This is it."

There was only one building in sight, an ugly erection which looked to have grown out of the drab, inhospitable landscape with its gable end on to another narrow lane joining the one they were on at the precise spot where the car had stopped.

They got out of the car, thanking the driver and moved slowly towards the building only about ten yards down the lane. Once on the lane, their view of all but its roof was hidden by the high wall beside the road.

"Will someone tell me what we are intending to do?" David asked sarcastically. "Knock at the door and demand the letter?"

"Ssh," Liz reproved. "There might be someone behind the wall."

They stopped under the end wall of the house, a foot or so short of a window with peeling paintwork, the right hand side of which was swinging open in a slight breeze. There were no sounds from inside.

There was a tight thumping in Liz's chest. Had they come so far in their quest for Christopher's freedom only to be thwarted? Desperation lent rashness to her and she edged closer to the window. David tried to pull her back but she shook him off, after which he stood with his back to the wall and a look of utter resignation on his face. Liz cautiously advanced so that she could see a tiny part of the room. Bit by bit she worked herself forward until the whole of the room was in view.

Suddenly she turned an animated face to the others, almost knocking Paul, close behind her, over in her excitement, and nearly inarticulate.

"It . . . it . . . it's *there!*" she stammered, wide eyed. "On the desk. A blue sheet of paper with a blue envelope. I know it's the same as . . . I saw Tony . . . And . . . there's no-one in the room."

Almost before they knew what was happening, Paul had pushed in front and was halfway in through the open window. David grabbed at him, but Liz was in the way and his brother dropped nimbly inside, leaving them horror stricken outside.

David pushed Liz to one side. "Paul!" he cried. "Come out of there at once! Do you hear me!"

"Someone else will!"

David was standing quite openly at the window and he saw his young brother grab the letter, thrust it into its envelope and turn back to the window. At that moment a look of dismay crossed his face and he glanced towards a door at the far side of the room. Quick as lightening, Paul pushed the letter behind a picture on the wall just beside him. He was not a moment too soon. The door opened and Paul could do nothing to avoid capture. David, who had been unable to take his eyes from the scene, knew that he was spotted, too. The man entering the room gave an angry exclamation, grabbing Paul by the scruff of the neck, and his cry brought another man into the room. David was not surprised to see that the second man was Moustache.

"Scram! Quick!" David hissed between clenched teeth to Alan and Liz. "We're seen."

Liz nodded, her hand to her mouth in the horror of their predicament.

There was no cover the way they had come, so Liz and Alan ducked below the window level and threw themselves towards the far side of the house. They dashed desperately past the main vehicle entrance which apparently led to the front door. The wall beside the road was lower here and over it they could see into an overgrown shrubbery. It was the only place that might provide any cover for them. Feverishly they dived for a little, arched gateway several yards further on from the main entrance, from whence it was but a step to the inside of an ancient yew tree.

"Not a bad place," Alan whispered, "but get behind me, Liz. Your red anorak will give us away. Someone's come out."

That 'someone' was Moustache who had come out in pursuit of David. The latter, too concerned about Paul's safety to care much about his own for once, offered no resistance but allowed Moustache to escort him inside.

"It was a good job David warned us to disappear," Liz whispered. "A few more seconds and we would all have been caught. It is bad enough as it is, but that would have been worse. The tragedy is that if Paul got the letter, they'll soon get it back again now."

"And once they've got it, they'll no doubt destroy

it," Alan added gruffly. "I hope they don't know there are four of us."

"Moustache would have recognised the two of us from the train," Liz answered in a low, thoughtful voice, "but I doubt if he ever saw us with David and Paul, so there is no reason for him to suspect they aren't on their own. — Unless anyone in the front of the house saw us dive past the main gates. We will assume not, for no-one has come looking for us. Let's hope David and Paul don't give us away."

"They won't do that. They'll know that two live fighters are worth more than four captives."

'You are probably right. Oh, what a mess I have got us into!" Liz groaned. "It's up to us now. But listen, Alan. When we decide what to do, we must act singly, so that there is still one of us in reserve."

"What can we do?"

Liz remained silent. She hadn't an answer to that question yet.

Alan asked another question in the same semi-audible whisper. "Do you think they'll report them to the police for breaking in?"

"I don't think so," Liz replied. "If they are crooks, that's the last thing they'll want to do. They'd be afraid of what the boys might tell — for they don't know how much they know. If the letter is an open secret, they'll wonder how much more is. I imagine it must be quite a shock to them to discover that David and Paul knew where to find them. It's not that I'm most worried about . . . "

"But?"

"As far as these criminals are concerned, the boys would be better out of the way completely."

She felt him stiffen and shiver.

"Liz, God wouldn't let that happen, would he?" His voice was pleading.

Doubt had crept into Liz's mind. She had thought ill of David for his temerity, but had there been some other way all the time?

"Perhaps I shouldn't have . . . " she began wearily. "But He's in control in spite of our mistakes. Dad once said he didn't believe in second causes. However, it is now our responsibility to use our heads and do all we can."

"If only we knew what was going on in there!"

"Well, one thing is certain. We are not going back to that window, for there is no cover there at all."

"What time is it?"

"Half past three."

"Ought one of us to go seeking a telephone?"

"I don't think so — not yet, at least. It might be ages before we came to a village or a house with a phone in this kind of country, and anything might happen here in that time. We could both be needed where we are."

Alan did not question Liz's authority. He knew that one of them had to make the decisions and that Liz was the quicker thinking of the two of them, a thing which counted in a situation like this.

They had not realised from the road just how large a house Crow End was. Now, peering at it through the dense foliage, they could see its length with several built on sections which gave the whole thing an ungainly, spidery appearance. Two ragged old pines stood between the house and the shrubbery like shabby sentinels. They might be useful as a means of concealment, Liz pondered. Outside the huge front door stood the blue car which had driven Moustache away from the station.

Liz's thoughts were suddenly interrupted when Moustache appeared outside again, staring curiously around as if looking for something — or someone. Did that mean that the two inside had split on them — perhaps in a boast that the men would not get away with it? However, Moustache soon went back inside, apparently satisfied that all was in order.

But the feeling of panic stayed with Liz. She or Alan would have to do something, and the sooner they did it the better. Presumably there were at least two men in the house. She knew that Moustache was there, and she assumed that so, too, was Joe to whom Moustache had been instructed to give the letter. It was possibly Joe's car and Joe's house, but it was equally possible that there were more than two men there. Certainly, she knew that later on Tony Masterson was coming after first making the other call for 'the boss'.

"If David and Paul don't come out soon, one of us will have to go in to find out what is happening," she whispered to her brother.

Alan nodded bravely. If the letter had been

156

retrieved from Paul there was no point in the men detaining the Ransoms — unless mischief were intended upon them. It was up to them to find out.

"We can't afford to wait too long," she added.

Her brother nodded again. "I'll go if you like," he volunteered reluctantly. "You'd know better what to do if I got caught as well."

"But you'll have to think for yourself if you go in," she told him. "I can't tell you what would happen or what you would need to do. It would depend entirely upon what you found."

"I'm ready."

They waited a few minutes more, then Liz said, "Now," when there had still been no signs of movement at the house, and certainly no uncere-monious ejection of David and Paul.

"I'll try to get round the back," Alan said, for he had been thinking it out. "It is too exposed for comfort to approach from this side."

It was Liz's turn to nod. "Be careful," she told him.

"I'll be careful," he promised.

Chapter 12

David allowed himself to be shepherded into the house by a growling Moustache. A sense of futility settled on him and he felt he no longer cared what happened. His only strong emotion was against Liz for bringing them there. The knowledge that she had not done it on her own behalf in no way lessened his resentment. Of one thing he was certain — he would put Paul's safety first.

David's first glimpse of Paul was of a grimly determined boy staring defiantly into the big man's face. That big man looked up at their entrance.

"Here's the other one, Joe," Moustache said giving David a helping shove into the room.

"Where's the letter?" Joe barked at David.

"Letter? What letter?" David asked, playing for time but knowing the question to be a futile one. "You can't detain us here. Leave my brother alone. Come on, Paul."

Paul did not move, but the two men did. Exchanging quick glances, Joe went to the window, closed — and to David's surprise — padlocked it, while Moustache similarly secured the door.

"Not so fast," Joe reproved David. "If you come snooping around private houses and think you can remove whatever you like, the least you can do is have a friendly little chat when the owner catches you!"

"You've no right . . . "

"Oh, but I have. Every right. You were caught trespassing. I've a good mind to send for the police."

"Suits us," said David, calling his bluff. "They'd like to see that letter."

The arrow hit, and the war was in the open from that moment. Maybe it hadn't been in their own interest for David to confirm their knowledge of the letter's importance. His intention had been to defend their vulnerable position, but he had only succeeded in making it even more vulnerable.

"Are there any more of you?" Joe demanded sourly.

"There might be half a dozen," David replied evasively. "If there are, you haven't a hope of deterring our purpose. We might even have informed the police where we were coming and why. Now, will you kindly let us go?"

"Give me that letter and you can go."

"It's . . . "

"David!" Paul shouted. "We haven't come so far

159

just to give in! Think of Christopher . . . and Liz."

Paul did not say the last bit reprovingly, but David felt the full force of a reproof.

"You were saying?" Joe prompted him.

David shook his head. It was no use denying knowledge of the letter again, for it was all too obvious that that was what they had come for. Anyway, they probably knew too much to expect immediate release.

Joe turned to Moustache. "Go and see if there are any more snoopers around," he ordered, "and telephone the boss to tell him exactly what has happened. He might want to abandon the place sooner than planned. It's obviously not safe any longer."

He turned back to the Ransoms as Moustache went without question to the door, unlocked it, went out and locked it again behind him.

"If you don't tell me where that letter is, we have ways and means of finding out," he threatened melodramatically. He was looking directly at David, recognising in him the greater measure of indecision, but David remained sullenly silent.

Joe turned his attention to Paul who had one pocket which bulged. He knew that the lad was the only one who had touched the letter, and the most likely place for it was in his pocket.

"Turn that pocket out," he commanded, not yet really worried at not retrieving the missing document.

Paul obligingly complied, pulling out a now

crumpled comic, his mother's letter which he should have posted, and a sundry collection of boy's bits and pieces. Joe threw the comic on the floor. Paul retrieved it reverently, while the big man grabbed for the letter. He slit it open and David wondered disdainfully how he imagined the letter he was seeking had got inside a sealed envelope.

"Dear Mother," Joe read. With a gesture of annoyance, he scanned the page then threw that away, too. Incongruously, David felt like laughing.

Joe took little notice as Paul leaned down and scooped up the discarded letter, replaced it in the envelope and pushed it back into his pocket, wrapped in the middle of the precious comic. The man was debating with himself. Was this strong willed, resolute lad most likely to succumb to threats or promises? Suddenly, he grabbed Paul by his shirt collar and shook the boy until his teeth rattled.

"What have you done with it?" he snarled, his patience ebbing.

"Hey, stop that!" David cried angrily, to be rewarded with a violent blow which sent him reeling into the wall.

"You'll get more than that if you don't co-operate!" Joe shouted roughly. "It isn't pleasant being made to talk, either for the one concerned or for the one watching," he said looking pointedly at David, who flushed with understanding and anger.

"You are wasting your time," Paul stated calmly and deliberately, also glancing at his brother in challenge, "for we will *not* talk!"

"We'll see about that," Joe replied ominously, and he proceeded to search Paul very roughly and extremely thoroughly. David looked on, all the time on the point of revealing the hiding place of the wanted document, in spite of Paul's determination. Joe, seeming to sense that the rougher he treated Paul the more likely David was to speak, deliberately worked to that end. Paul knew that David was wavering and shook his head at him, wishing that his brother had never seen him hide it. The big man jerked him round so that his back was to David. The thorough search convinced Joe that the letter was not on Paul's person. Tension was beginning to show on his face, for he had been sure that Paul had the letter hidden on him. The contents of that piece of paper must indeed be incriminating to account for the hint of fear glinting in his eyes. David stood with clenched hands, admiring his young brother's courage and yet full of indecision himself. He could see that Paul was trying to ignore Joe's threats and thinking hard, but David knew they would not be able to hold out indefinitely. The men's patience would only last so long, then they would begin to apply *real* pressure. So was there any point in prolonging the issue and maybe getting hurt? It was surely more than even Christopher would expect. But Liz would find it hard to forgive him, and that mattered. There was no harm in playing for just a little more time and allowing Joe to search him, too. After all, the other two were outside and might be enlisting the aid of some passing motorist . . .

David knew that Paul feared he might betray them at any minute. He was therefore not surprised when the boy began strange antics the moment Joe transferred his attention to him, though he could not imagine what his objective was. As Joe roughly began to turn out every pocket and examine every possible hiding place on David's person, the first thing to catch his attention from the younger boy was a scarcely audible 'Psst', as if trying to catch the other's attention. He spun round and struck out, narrowly missing the boy and held on to David with a vice-like grip as he turned to glare at Paul, but the lad had assumed an attitude of wide-eyed inno-cence. David was annoyed when Paul repeated the sound. He could only make a bad situation worse by his fooling, whether or not he had his reasons. The man's own intense annoyance only seemed to drive Paul on to open gesticulations as if he would convey some secret message to his brother, but giving up abruptly the moment he caught Joe's eye.

"Quit fooling, Paul," David snapped. "We are in enough trouble already."

Desperation flashed across Paul's face for a second.

"You'll get a belt over the ear if you don't," Joe warned.

Paul ignored his threat and promptly appeared to go beserk. From that moment, the search was interrupted by low whispers from Paul to David, whispers not quite loud enough to be heard, but noticeable enough to increase Joe's anger to fury point. At the same time the boy began to dance around the other two, physically harrassing Joe by tugging at a sleeve, grabbing at his hair or dancing behind his back and swinging round his neck. Joe abruptly let go of David and gave Paul a stinging blow on the side of his face.

"Don't say I didn't warn you," he barked, approaching Paul with his hand raised to strike again, but the other staggered away round the centre table, his face red but leering at his pursuer as if he were mad, easily evading the bigger, clumsier figure as he danced about the room. David stood hypnotised, half inclined to laugh hysterically and yet trembling with anger at Paul's outrageous behaviour. Joe returned to him and dragged him towards the door.

"Next door, you, and don't try any funny tricks, either of you!"

At once David came back to life and he made a valiant effort at resistance. It was no use. Joe had twice the weight and strength of the slim David, and he had to go. Paul made no further effort to come near them and David's last glimpse of his face as he went out revealed an expression of entire satisfaction in spite of an obviously painful face which he held with one hand. David could only guess as to what he was up to, and he had no time to speak or frown any warning.

Paul waited only to hear the key turn in the lock before he moved. He only needed a minute on his own to do what he wanted. His scheme, born of desperation, had worked even if it had cost him a sore face. Moustache might come back, so he quickly and silently did what he had planned, with a fervent, whispered, "Please let it be the right thing to do."

By the time David was thrust back into the room, Paul was apparently just as they had left him. Both Joe and David glanced sharply in his direction. His face was quite expessionless.

Joe did not come in this time but locked them together in the room and departed without another word. "Did he find it?" Paul asked with a lopsided smile.

"Funny boy!" David replied, gentler than he might otherwise because of his brother's obvious pain.

They didn't feel like talking. It was no use planning, anyway. All they could do was wait and see what happened. David didn't question Paul for fear of eavesdroppers and he knew that he would only find out what his brother wanted him to know!

"I hope Liz and Alan don't get caught," Paul said quietly in a while but David put a warning finger to his lips and pointed at the door. Paul nodded but felt sure his voice had not been loud enough to be heard.

In the silence, they examined their surroundings. The room was large, easily accommodating the heavy, old fashioned furniture. There was a massive dresser containing cracked and dusty plates, a desk, a table and several chairs. Opposite the window was a fireplace without a fire. The only luxury in the room was an enormous, but now shabby, Indian carpet stretching almost from wall to wall. They were not surprised to see that there was no telephone on the desk. The window had a deep recess with a seat of the same dark wood as the rest of the furniture.

"Could we . . . break out?" Paul whispered, pondering the window with its padlock.

"Not a chance," David replied. We'd have to smash it and they'd hear us and get us again. The only thing we'd gain would be a lot of cuts."

Before long, both Joe and Moustache arrived back with faces as black as thunder. Having searched the boys to no purpose they now turned their attention to the room itself, seeking in and around the furniture and behind the curtains. They moved cushions, mats and books and did not bother to put them back. Paul wondered if Joe's wife would have to do that. The brothers remained silent in the face of fresh questions and harassment, which increased as the men's tempers became shorter. Even Paul did not dare to provoke them any further, for fear of the situation becoming really ugly. Everywhere the search proved abortive. Joe and Moustache looked just about everywhere but behind the pictures on the walls.

Suddenly, a telephone shrilled in a distant part of the house and both men left the room.

"Probably the boss to tell them what to do with

us," Paul laughed a little shakily.

David frowned at him. "I don't know how you can see anything funny in the situation at all," he grumbled. "I don't know who is the more stupid, Liz or you! You were mad to jump in here. You both act before you think. It is only a matter of time and they will get that letter back, then we will be no better off for all this." He spread his hands helplessly. "And they will probably sue us for breaking in."

"They will only find out where the letter is if *you* tell them, David," Paul said looking his brother straight in the eye. "You forget that Liz and Alan will be doing something."

David shrugged impatiently. "Tell me, just tell me what they can do in a way out place like this. There probably isn't a phone for miles. Have you noticed it is coming dusk out there now? Soon it will be night. What will they do then? Freeze to death! If only I'd . . . "

The brothers jumped when a gentle tapping sounded at the door, and they were astounded to hear Alan's whisper.

David sprang across the room and put his mouth to the keyhole.

"Alan? Liz?"

"Just Alan, David," came the reply. "I'll have to be quick in case they come back. There doesn't seem to be anyone else in the house but Moustache and another man. I've been hiding, waiting for them to go away, but they're bound to see me here if they come back. Have you got the letter?''

"Yes."

"What are they going to do?''

We haven't the faintest. So far, they've just searched us.''

"Liz said she and I had to act independently — just in case. She is still outside. What shall I do? Do you know where they keep the key for this door?''

"In their pockets,'' David whispered back, thinking quickly all the time. "The important thing is that we get a message out, and that means finding a phone. Do you think you dare have a look round? Take your time and wait until you are sure you're safe. There'll probably be more than one in this house. Ring the police . . . No, I've a better idea. Ring Dr. Mason. He knows the whole background and he will have more time to talk to them and would no doubt get a better hearing than you, too. Ask him — but he'll know what to do and say. Remember, this is Crow End and the station was Blossom Bridge. He'll no doubt ring home, too. Be off before they catch you, Alan and — mind how you go.''

There was a muffled swish as Alan moved away and then silence again. They looked at each other. David was smiling.

"At last,'' he said, "I begin to feel a little hope. Dr. Mason will organise everything. We can trust him to do his part, if Alan can manage to do his.''

"You're trusting the wrong person,'' Paul murmured, but David's thoughts were elsewhere

and he was not listening, so Paul sighed and said no
more.

Chapter 13

Liz was so cold that she felt she had set into stone. The road was very close behind her, so she dare not make a noise by rubbing her hands or stamping her feet to improve the circulation. She did her best to forget her cold, stiff limbs by considering their problems and planning ahead.

It seemed hours since Alan had left her. In fact, dusk had fallen since then and she could no longer see the house as clearly. She dare not move any nearer, however, for if — when — Alan returned, he had to find her. She wondered how long she had to wait before assuming that he had been captured, too. There had been no movements at all since Moustache had taken that perfunctory look around, but she guessed there had been plenty of activity inside. Had Paul managed to get hold of that letter when he jumped into the room? She didn't know, for only David had been looking in through the window at the time. If he had, it seemed impossible to hope that he could have retained it. In which case, they were no better off.

Liz felt suddenly alone and depressed. For the first time she began to question whether she had been right to take so much upon herself on Christopher's behalf, at the same time dragging all the others into it. There was no denying that it had brought them into a perilous situation, a situation too great for them, and from which it seemed impossible to extricate themselves. This place was so remote that the crooks they were dealing with could get away with anything . . . A wave of fear spread over her. It was fear for her family and friends more than for herself. In fact, the others were in a worse position than she was. It seemed ironic that she was the instigator of today's escapade and she was the only one who was still free if Alan . . .

With a symbolic gesture she turned her face up to the sky, now spread with the purple hue of evening like a ceiling a few inches above the dark foliage over her head, reminding herself that they were not alone. So, they had problems? They were not the first to have them, and problems were not solved by avoiding them. They were solved by going through them, as the Israelites had gone through the Red Sea. 'When thou comest to the waters, thou shalt not go down but through,' the poet had para-phrased God's message through Isaiah to the people. "And by His help, we'll go through our

'Red Sea'," Liz told herself firmly. "The enemy might be in front of us and the enemy behind us, but they hardly add up to an Egyptian army — and they were overthrown! If only good might come out of evil and David might be spoken to through it all!"

Now feeling much more optimistic, she tried to decide what to do if Alan did not return to her soon. Rather than cut off their last life-line, she would avoid going into the house after them but take to the road in search of another house which had a telephone. She would just have to trust that she set off in the right direction. She would contact the local police somehow or other and tell them the situation. Even if the boys no longer had the document which apparently could prove Christopher's innocence, the authorities surely would not view with favour the forceful detaining of three young people against their wishes at Crow End, even though one was guilty of illegal entry. Their story might at least lead the police to look again into Christopher's case.

A gentle rustling nearby interrupted her thoughts. To her intense relief she saw the dark form of Alan approaching her straggly yew tree hiding place.

"Mission accomplished!" he whispered jubilantly when he reached her side. "They've got the letter — though how they've managed to keep it I haven't a clue — and I've managed to telephone Dr. Mason, who has promised to contact the police and our folks."

"Great!" Liz exclaimed more loudly than she

intended in her relief. The cheering news made her forget how cold she was. "Tell me what happened . . . but quickly."

"I'm afraid it took me a long time," her brother began apologetically. He felt rather than saw Liz's nod of the head.

"I thought they'd got you."

"Sorry," Alan said feelingly, then continued. "I knew I couldn't afford to be careless. It wasn't too easy to get to the door at the back of the house, and I'm afraid I did have to take one or two risks. The shrubs go quite near to the gable end of the building, but the back is as open as this side . . . lawns at one time, I guess. It was still light then, of course, and I waited ages to make sure no-one was about before I made each move. I eventually decided to keep close to the house wall, ducking under the windows as I passed by. That was done in one quick dash and my worst moment was as I reached the porch outside the door. I stood pressed into the corner of the two walls when I heard someone come to the door. They were just through the wall from me. If they'd come forward a yard, they could not have missed seeing me. I can tell you I thought they would hear my heartbeats! Then the door closed again and there was silence, which told me that the person had gone back inside. You can imagine how much I wanted to go through that door! I really thought at that moment that I couldn't go on with it."

"Poor Alan. Go on. What happened when you

173

did?'' Liz asked, trying to hurry up the narrative.

"I was in a long hallway with clothes hanging from pegs all the length of one wall. These proved a very good hiding place when I heard someone coming again.''

"Poor Alan,'' Liz murmured again sympathetically, squeezing his arm. "How nerve racking!''

"Yes. You know I'm not really one for adventures. It put years on me.'' He paused. "Listen, Liz. There's a car coming.''

The sound of an engine drew nearer, the headlights casting a white beam into the sky then on the rough grass in the fields further on the lane, and the car roared past without pausing at the big, broad gateway of Crow Edge.

"That's the first car to go past since we got here,'' Liz said. "It was a bit too early for a police car to get here, I suppose. Go on, Alan, before they do come.''

"No-one came into the hall, but I heard talking through an open door at the far end. One voice was saying that the boss had instructed them to prepare to move out to somewhere I did not catch and they had to forget the job they had planned for that night. I think the gang must have been planning to steal the Crown jewels tonight, judging by the men's annoyance. Anyway, it was obviously their biggest job yet. I can tell you, we're not very popular for sticking our noses in! Also, the boss had apparently told them to make sure they got that letter back, or else, but that the two lads hadn't to be harmed. Their own view was that a little bit of arm

174

twisting was all that was needed to make David squeal, but they didn't seem to dare, after what the Big White Chief had said. After that they drifted away, and I cautiously followed the direction of their voices until I realised I could also hear David and Paul. It was quite easy to work out which room they were in, but I had to find somewhere to hide until the men left it. There was a cupboard nearby and, by doubling myself in two, I managed to get inside. A distant phone rang and both men hurried away, so I took my chance straight away. There might have been someone else with David and Paul, but I'd to risk that. The door was locked, of course, so we talked through the keyhole. David said they had the letter and told me what to do. Finding a telephone in the house was, to my surprise, about the easiest part of the whole thing as there was one in the first room I tried. Dr. Mason sounded quite stupified at first, then I thought he sounded amused. No wonder! It does all seem incredulous! I only had time to give him a quick resume, but he soon grasped what had happened and said not to worry, for he would take care of the situation for us. He told me to be sure I wasn't caught, too. David was right. It would have taken far too long to explain everything to the police, whereas I only needed to tell Dr. Mason where we were and why, in about one sentence."

"I dread to think what opinion he must have of me, leading you all into this!"

"I tell you I didn't go into details. I don't think I

175

mentioned anyone's name — except mine, when I was saying who was speaking. I just said 'we', that we were in trouble at a place called Crow End, near Blossom Bridge, after chasing a letter that could have helped Christopher. He said he knew of the place, and that was when he told me not to worry. Then he was just asking me another question when I heard sounds again somewhere near and had to get out quickly. How long do you think the police will be?"

"Not long, surely. They'll have to get in touch with the local men, that's all. I hope they do come soon. I'm frozen."

Moving quietly, Alan removed his jacket and offered it to her. "Put this on top of yours. I'm quite warm after all the activity, but I can hear your teeth chattering."

Liz took it gratefully without argument. She did not want to end up with pneumonia to remember the evening by. "If you can hear them, others might," she agreed with a feeble attempt at lightheartedness. "Alan, how had they managed to hang on to that letter?"

Her brother shook his head. "We'd not time to go into that."

During this long, scarcely audible conversation, they had kept their eyes focussed, between heavy branches, on the grey house in front. Gradually, more and more lights had been turned on and there were sounds, even at this distance, of intense activity.

"Perhaps they'll do a bunk and just abandon David and Paul."

They were quiet for a while, then Liz whispered, "Don't dash out as soon as a car comes, Alan, in case it is the wrong one. Wait until we can see it is a police car. Someone else might come first. For instance, we know that Tony Masterson should be arriving this evening." She sighed. "I wish they would be quick."

Expecting, as they were, aid any minute, the time dragged interminably. The two of them huddled together in an attempt to conserve body heat, sitting on the dry carpet of leaves dropped over many years from the branches around them. They heard an owl hooting in the shrubbery to their left, the minute scutterings of little nocturnal creatures, the odd swish of breeze in the branches, the muffled sounds of activity from the house, but the only traffic they heard was far away in the distance.

"I wouldn't have known this was an overpopulated island if they hadn't told me," Liz giggled suddenly and, as Alan hastily hushed her," she whispered, "I promise I'm not going hysterical! But it's so cold I don't know whether to laugh or cry."

"All this waiting and solitude is enough to get on our nerves. My inside is tied in hard knots," Alan sympathised, then he groaned, "I can't understand why the police are so long in coming. They'll let those crooks get away yet."

"Hush, Alan. Don't get despondent. They'll come, just you see."

Alan nodded in the darkness. "But I can't understand . . . " he repeated. His thoughts continued as his voice broke off, then he eventually finished, "I don't think we are anywhere near to the real explanation, even yet."

"Oh, Alan, it's surely simple now, as far as we are concerned! Christopher has got blamed for what this gang has done. All we need to do is to show the letter to the police when they get here, and he's free. I don't mind admitting I'd like to see what it says, too!"

"Ssh! You're probably right, but from the beginning nothing has turned out as we've expected. Strange. And this Tony Masterson must be the strangest man alive — he'll turn out to be the big boss yet! . . . Sorry, I don't really believe that."

"I should think not. Lester Addison seems to be the one most likely to know something about what happened. Working at the jewellers, he knew about the diamonds and we know he has been in contact with Moustache. Oh, never mind the details! I'm only bothered about Christopher, so I'll not worry my head about . . . "

She broke off suddenly as the house door opened. Both Joe and Moustache came out, their arms laden with packages which they flung into the back of the car and went in again.

"Oh, *please* hurry!" Alan pleaded with the absent but long expected police car.

"Most worthwhile things have to be waited for — or fought for," Liz replied reflectively after a pause

178

and wondered for a moment why Alan chuckled. "Sorry, did I sound like Dad?"

"No harm in that," he whispered back, "but you even used his tone of voice! Liz, I don't mind admitting that I wish Dad were here at this very moment. He's so wise and . . . and sensible."

A pale crescent moon came riding into the clear sky above the house roof. They watched as it rose higher until they felt that the rest of their lives must be spent waiting, waiting. Joe and Moustache continued to appear from time to time, and by now the car was almost crammed full.

"You were right, Alan, they are going to do a bunk."

As soon as Liz had spoken, Moustache came out once more, this time with only a small case in his hand. This he pushed with difficulty in the already overloaded car and, without a backward glance he started the engine and drove away.

After he had gone, the night sounds seemed magnified in the stillness. The owl population was obviously more numerous than the human, thereabouts, and the doleful bleat of sheep in the rough fields seemed very near.

"The night must have warmed up a little, or I've got used to it."

"I'm more hungry than cold," Alan replied. "It was fortunate we left our shopping in David's office, but I could eat some of the biscuits in it right now."

Liz realised with surprise that they had missed

two meals. It was the first time she had thought about food.

But thoughts of food were abruptly abandoned as, almost without warning, an arc of light threw the branches above them into bright relief against the dark sky, and a car turned in at the gates, skidding to a halt where the blue one had been. Almost before the engine had stopped, the driver seemed to be getting out.

"Stay here. It doesn't look like a police car."

The man cast a long shadow on the ground as he hurried to the door. There was something vaguely familiar about his shape and movements, but it was not Tony Masterson. It was Dr. Mason. In their surprise and delight they did not stop to ponder his boldness in so openly drawing up in front of the house. Getting ready to vacate their hiding place, it occurred to Liz first that it was a dangerous thing for the doctor to do. They couldn't be sure there was only one man left in the house, and another was on his way here. If they were armed, Dr. Mason stood no chance.

"Shall we go?" Alan asked, conscious of Liz's restraining hand.

"I think you'd better go on your own again," she said with reluctance. "You know where David and Paul are . . . were . . . and he'll expect you to be around somewhere. Don't let on that I'm here — yet, anyway, in case the men get to know. You *and* Dr. Mason might come croppers, too. He isn't being careful enough. Go back to the road through that little door and join him from the main gate, then no-one will know where you were hiding. Go on, Alan. We should be alright, now, but we can't afford to relax."

Alan left Liz reluctantly. His part that evening had been an unenviable one, but hers more so. Knowing his sister, he realised how difficult it must have been for her to endure inaction and stand in one spot almost freezing to death for so long.

"Go on," she repeated, knowing what he was thinking. "I'm alright — really."

Alan caught Dr. Mason up before he had made any move on the doorstep. It was almost as if he had been waiting for him, for he was merely standing there facing the wooden door.

"Good lad, Alan," Dr. Mason said warmly. "You did well to get in touch with me. I suppose we'd better be quiet in case we are heard. Come on, let's find those adventurers!"

Alan followed him as if in a dream. There was a sense of unreality about the confident Dr. Mason, the silent house and the way in which he was able to lead the older man to the room where the captives waited.

"It's that room at the end of the passage," Alan whispered, "but it's locked."

"Could be a problem," the other admitted, "but I've managed to procure some master keys, so let's keep our fingers crossed."

In the same uncanny, conjuring like fashion, Dr. Mason selected a key from the bunch, fitted it in the lock and opened the door at the first attempt.

"Good," Dr. Mason exclaimed in satisfaction. "That was a fortunate choice." He winked conspiringly at Alan.

As the door opened, they saw David and Paul sitting there, silent and depressed. Then the captives looked up in amazement and sprang to their feet. David's whole demeanour spelled welcome and relief.

"What . . . ? How . . . ?" He laughed. "Are we glad to see you! I don't know how you got in, but now that you have, let's all get out."

Dr. Mason smiled genially at them all. Only Paul's expression was enigmatic. His initial smile had faded, and he was staring at him with something akin to shock in his eyes. Dr. Mason was surprised at his slowness to respond, which was not like the boy, but he was young and the experience must have been an ordeal. Without hurry, the older man perched his attractive, slender figure on the arm of a chair and put a finger to his lips.

"We are in enemy territory, remember," he reminded them for David, in his relief, had raised his voice. "We could be interrupted at any minute, so we have no time to stand on ceremony. We are all together, so we will stay together and make a dash for it in a moment. By the way, where is the irrepressible Elizabeth — I can't imagine her consenting to being left behind!"

Remembering Liz's injunction, Alan replied before any of the others could do so. "We don't tell her everything! This is no sort of escapade to drag a girl into!''

"She went shopping into Town," Paul added firmly with unflinching gaze and a definiteness which surprised them all.

It was true, it was *all* true, except for the implication that Liz alone had gone shopping. David opened his mouth to speak but closed it again. Something about his brother restrained him. Young Paul had something distressing on his mind. He was uncertain and agitated, his hands clenched into hard bulges in his pockets.

Laughter lines crinkled the corners of Dr. Mason's eyes. "You'll be in for it when she finds out she has missed all the fun," he teased, and David wished he would hurry, as he had said they should. As if reading his thoughts, Dr. Mason went on, "But we've all got to get out of here, plus that letter you told me about, Alan, which I presume you still have." He saw David's quick nod. "You are to be complimented on a smart piece of work. I confess I am intrigued to know how you have concealed it until now, for 'they' have no doubt conducted quite a thorough search," he added with a wry smile at the chaotic condition of the room. Sensing their restlessness, he stood up. "Yes, we'd better get a move on. I'll tell you what I suggest, and then you can decide if you like the idea. The nearest police station is a mile or so beyond Blossom Bridge Station. If you were to hand over this letter to me, I could take it straight there, dropping you at the station on the way."

"We surely need to go with you," David objected.

"Not necessarily," the doctor replied pleasantly. "You've all gone through enough already and I think I am completely in the picture. Besides, the last train runs through Blossom Bridge." He consulted his watch, "in a little more than half an hour. Best get home and set your family's minds at rest. I'm afraid I hadn't time to give them many details, but that you were alright. If we do as I suggest, it is highly unlikely that these crooks can get away before the police come to round them up, should they discover your escape."

"Wouldn't it have been better to contact the police, instead of coming yourself?" Paul interrupted gruffly, and David was annoyed with his brother for bringing a brief frown of aggravation to the doctor's forehead.

The smile returned to Dr. Mason's face. "By tomorrow you'll be thanking me for taking over for you." he assured them. "Tired and hungry as you all are, I should think the last thing you want is a night of questions and cross questions."

David's mind was made up. "It's a good idea," he agreed, "and we have no time to argue about it. I've had enough. Give Dr. Mason the letter, Paul,"

Paul did not move. He cast an appealing glance at David then his mouth set in a stubborn line and he shook his head. Annoyed, David pushed impatiently past him to get it himself, but Paul grabbed him by the arm and hung on like a leech.

"Wait!" he cried, and he was trembling. "I know we're short of time, but there's a question I'd like to ask."

David tried to shake him off. "It'll wait. We've *got* to . . . "

"It won't wait," Paul insisted, "and you'll soon see why." He turned to their genial rescuer. "Dr. Mason, have you ever been inside Christopher's flat?"

"You know he hasn't — he told us that, before."

"Please, David!" Paul pleaded. "Dr. Mason?"

"David's right, Paul," Dr. Mason replied humouringly. "I always meant to call on Christopher but I'm afraid I never did."

"We're wasting time. Either get that letter, or let me get it, Paul," David ordered.

Paul stubbornly stood his ground. "I have some property of yours to return, Dr. Mason." He drew from his pocket a very dirty handkerchief which he began to unknot. "I notice that one of your cuffs is buttoned, while you have had to use cuff links on the other sleeve, so you will no doubt be extremely glad to get your missing button back. With Christopher's compliments — from his kitchen floor." He turned to the others in the bewildered silence. "I found this the night we searched the flat — and I don't think there will be many buttons like this missing from men's shirts! How do you think it got there, Dr. Mason?"

They all regarded the wheel button in his hand and the identical ones on the doctor's shirt as if mesmerised. The man took the button, his face emotionless. That it matched the others was useless to deny.

"I haven't a clue, Constable," he said lightly, ruffling Paul's hair to his annoyance. "Does that make me suspect number one?"

"Yes, exactly what are you implying?" David challenged Paul.

"Paul is understandably overwrought," Dr. Mason defended him, "and to someone with such detective genius" — he smiled at Paul — "this button is indeed incriminating evidence. I wish I could tell you how it got there. It must have got into Christopher's stuff somehow, perhaps on one of his visits to me." He saw uncertainty still on the faces before him and, becoming brisk and businesslike, he added, "However, this is no time to let silly suspicions spoil our happy relationship. Let's take that letter and go."

David was even yet ready to respond to the appeal in Dr. Mason's soft spoken voice and his outstretched hand, but caution and distrust on the part of the other two made him hesitate. Dr. Mason was watching him and David suspected a gleam of challenge in the blue eyes.

Suddenly he felt a chill of apprehension. Paul would not lie. That button *had* been in Christopher's flat, and Dr. Mason had only a few minutes ago claimed never to have been there. Certainly, *someone* had seemed to keep one step ahead of them all the time, and only Dr. Mason had known what

186

they were doing. From the beginning he had been very insistent that he was kept informed of any development. Basically, they didn't really know much about him, except that he was obviously very wealthy and clever. Was he cleverer than they had realised before? As Dr. Mason continued to watch him, David realised the man had followed his train of thoughts correctly, for small beads of perspiration appeared at his temples. For a second, David felt the panic of an animal suddenly caught in a trap as it dawned on him that Dr. Mason had been in no real hurry ever since he joined them in this room. He had not seemed to feel any danger of being taken by surprise in someone else's house. He himself had heard Dr. Mason's car arrive, and yet there had been no investigations . . .

A sudden sound startled them all. It sounded like a car door being slammed. Dr. Mason's agitation was obvious now, and when he spoke his voice was harsh. "We must get out," he said urgently. "Don't you hear? — someone is coming. Quickly, the letter!"

"We are sorry, Dr. Mason," Alan replied quietly, "but we would rather not. You promised to help us, to get the help of the police, but you never did that. You walked in here as unconcernedly as if you knew the place and were expected . . . "

" . . . and we think that the only thing you are worried about is to get hold of that letter," Paul added defiantly.

"Really, you are the most infuriating stupids,"

Dr. Mason snapped. "I order you this minute . . ."

They remained unco-operative and stubborn. Then footsteps approached them down the corridor. The doctor's face darkened. Now his was the panic and the fact did not escape them. Before he could speak again, the door opened and in walked the grey, distinguished Tony Masterson, who stopped short in surprise on seeing the gathering in the room.

"Sorry, Boss," he said apologetically to Dr Mason. "You having a spot of trouble?" and he visibly started at the look of utter malevolence directed at him.

Chapter 14

The battle was in the open now. Suddenly a lot of mysteries had been cleared up, but that did not help their situation or Christopher's cause.

"Lenny's gone with the first lot of stuff to be disposed of in the usual way. I met him on my way here," Dr. Mason told Tony Masterson. "You'd better go and get Joe. Lock the door behind you," he said, flinging the handful of keys in his direction.

The truth had hit David like a stinging blow, and his crumpled esteem for Dr. Mason made him far more bitter than the others. Looking him in the eye he asked in cold fury as soon as Tony had gone, "You put those diamonds in Christopher's flat?"

Dr. Mason did not reply but looked away from the hatred in David's gaze.

David looked scarcely able to contain himself. "Judas!" he accused and Dr. Mason recoiled as if hit by a physical blow. "You pretend to help us and to

189

work with us, while all the time you're laughing at us, making sure we do not spoil your little game! We really put our heads in the noose when we rang you today, didn't we?" he ended bitterly.

Dr. Mason looked flushed and angry but did not reply.

"In fact, you no doubt knew we were here even before I rang you," Alan added, "because those two crooks had already phoned you. No wonder you approached Crow End so boldly. They already knew you were coming and had your instructions to keep out of the way. David's right, you've double crossed us. To think we expected you to go to the police!"

Dr. Mason gave an impatient gesture. "Listen, all of you," he replied quietly, but apparently addressing David in particular, as if to regain some of the latter's esteem of him. "I'm sorry it had to work out this way," he said. "Truly sorry. You deserve something better. But if you cast your minds back you will remember that I did my best to dissuade you from becoming involved at all, because I didn't want to have to work against you, or disillusion you."

"You didn't want us to get involved!" David retorted. "We were involved already, because Christopher was involved. You deliberately threw the blame on him then . . . "

"That was unfortunate." Dr. Mason still seemed reluctant to accept their censure. "Christopher was not meant to be implicated at all. That drawer was simply intended as a temporary hiding place."

"That was when you realized you were being followed." Paul added his contribution. "And I suppose that car was at the end of the lane at your orders watching our house to see if anyone came in answer to our advertisement, just in case we did not let you know. But why send Tony Masterson to pretend . . . ?" Dr. Mason did not deign to answer his questions. Instead, he spoke as if thinking aloud, seeking to justify his actions to himself as well as them. "In this world every man has to live for himself," he said. "You'll find out eventually. High ideals are uncomfortable companions. They get you nowhere and impress no-one. I have every admiration for you youngsters with your standards." He looked quizzically at David, "and regret to have to oppose you, but it's to be the best man who wins. And *that will be me*, make no mistake about that. I feel only regret that sometimes people get trodden on, but at times it is unavoidable. If they will throw themselves under one's feet . . . " He shrugged expressively.

In Alan's mind, disgust mixed with pity, and he knew he had to speak out. "I prefer Dad's philosophy, Dr. Mason," he replied. "It is because of selfishness and greed that this world is in the state it is, and God's disapproval is upon it. You were in the evening service only last week when Dad preached on the text, 'What is a man profited if he gain the whole world and lose his own soul?' The most important thing is to be right with God."

The door opened, bringing an end to the conversation. Tony Masterson entered, followed by Joe, who winked at Dr. Mason. The latter acknowledged them with a nod, then quietly but firmly addressed the three captives. "Now that we've had our little talk, I'm sorry but I must demand that letter. I don't know how you knew about it, but you were foolish to try to get your hands on it. If you imagine you can get out of this room with it you are mistaken. Hand it over."

Angry and disappointed, the youngsters shook their heads.

"Where have you looked for it?" Dr. Mason asked Joe.

The man answered with a kind of helpless gesture. "We looked everywhere. It isn't on them and it isn't in the room. And yet it must be because that older one," — he indicated David — "he wavered once or twice and almost spat it out."

David did not look at Dr. Mason who said nothing but by a single gesture of the hand indicated that they should be searched again. From time to time, as the man went systematically over them, Dr. Mason spoke in low, persuasive tones, promising to help find another way to exonerate Christopher if they would co-operate now, making sure that they realised that because of them he was having to clear out from the district sooner than he would have planned, in fact before his biggest task was completed, and again attempting to justify his way of life.

"You can't be a crook and yet object to being called one," David said bluntly in a tight voice.

At the same time, Paul's letter slipped out of his comic. Dr. Mason pounced but Joe merely shrugged.

"That won't help you," he told him, "unless you want to know about someone's new braces. 'Dear Mum,' it begins. I read it."

Paul watched without concern as Dr. Mason glanced at the feminine handwriting on the envelope, then he took it back as the other held it out to him.

"Then I'm afraid there is no alternative to this," Dr. Mason said with apparent regret and, to their horror, drew a small revolver from his pocket. Grabbing Paul in front of him, he held it to his back.

"No — don't move," he ordered as both David and Alan involuntarily took a step forward. Shaking, they stopped and their hands dropped to their sides. "I didn't want to have to make my point so forcibly, but I did say I must and *would* have that letter, and we've wasted enough time. I've always liked you lot and I'd hate to harm any of you, but if you insist on asking for it, I have no option — just as there was nothing I could do about Christopher's misfortune." He ignored David's derisive snort but turned to him as if recognising in him the weakest link. "Do I make myself clear?"

He waited while David fought the biggest mental battle of his life. His furious anger at Dr. Mason sealed his lips but his brother's position showed the risk to be too great. He did not believe that the man would shoot. Crook he might be, but David suspected he would stop short at murder. However, they had been surprised before!

"Don't, David. He won't shoot," Paul entreated, apparently thinking on the same lines as David. "Think of Christopher."

"I suggest you think of your brother," Dr. Mason corrected. "Christopher is in no danger where he is, and five years will soon go. But if I were to use this . . . " He did not need to finish.

"You . . . you . . . !" Dr. Mason knew that David had lost his battle. "It's behind that picture." The boy held his head in his hands.

"Very sensible," Dr. Mason said ingratiatingly, "as I'm sure the others will agree. — Joe, will you oblige?"

The letter was easy to retrieve now that they knew where to look for it. Joe soon had it in his hands. One glance sufficed to tell Dr. Mason that the writing on the blue envelope was his own.

"Very ingenious hiding place," he commended them. "You deserve to win but, regrettably, that cannot be allowed. Take it to the fireplace," he commanded, and it was Tony this time who complied. "Use those matches so conveniently sitting there, and let's put an end to this drama."

David, his head still in his hands, heard the strike of a match and saw the brightness of the flare of light between his fingers. In a matter of seconds, there were only ashes in the grate.

"There! I feel more comfortable now that that job's done," Dr. Mason breathed, pocketing his gun again. "I even feel inclined for benevolence. I'm sure these folks are hungry, Joe, for I suspect they've not eaten for a while. Go and rustle them some food up. I don't mind some myself, at the same time. Masterson, you go and make sure the girl isn't around. It's out of character for her to be left behind."

The men went without a word.

"We don't want any tea," Paul said flatly. "We'd rather go, if you don't mind."

"I'm afraid that is out of the question."

David looked up sharply. "You said we could go if we gave you the letter."

"But you didn't give it to me! I had to force it from you. You know too much. If I let you go, what would you do? You'd go back home and tell your folks all the details of your adventure. They, in turn, will go straight to the police with the same story and that doesn't quite give us time to clear out to safer places. So, again I am sorry, but we'll have to detain you a little longer."

"You can't do that! They'll be worried sick at home, whatever you told them."

"No doubt you decided to risk that when you set out on this foolish errand."

"Without the letter we have no evidence."

"I prefer to play safe. I don't know what you know."

Dr. Mason left them, too. They heard the dull

click of the lock as he turned the key.

"David, we don't blame you," Alan began as soon as they were alone, for the elder Ranson brother looked utterly depressed. "Christopher wouldn't have expected you to do otherwise."

David gave no indication that he had heard. Paul glanced at him as he once more carefully repacked his pockets. "Alan's right," he said. "We've done our best."

David could not explain that his had been a triple blow. They had risked so much on Christopher's behalf and failed, they in general and he in particular had been betrayed by one he had revered above all others and, lying in the debris of that betrayal was not only his crumpled idol but his own crumpled ideology, of which Dr. Mason had so much been the pattern. Others might have the same outlook on life and might also be able to add unselfishness to their qualities, but it was Dr Mason whom David had aped and trusted. If one man could prove to have feet of clay, so could they all. Dr. Mason cared only for himself. He did not hesitate to 'use' other people or remove them out of his way should he consider that necessary. David wanted to cry like a child.

"I almost hope they catch Liz now," Alan was whispering when David's mind came back to the present, his voice too low to be overheard. "She will catch cold out there, and she has nothing to eat. At least we are to be given free board, it seems."

"What you mean is," David said expressionlessly, "that since I have let you down, there's nothing we can do, there's nothing she can do, so we might as well sit down and die!"

"Stop it, David! We have been tricked by someone cleverer than us, that's all," Alan replied firmly, "and Liz won't blame you, anymore than we do."

David grunted and lapsed into silence again. It was alright for them. Their only disappointment was in carrying out an unsuccessful exercise, and theirs had been surprise rather than shock at Dr. Mason's involvement.

"It's difficult, somehow, to think of Dr. Mason as a criminal," Alan said meditatively, " — in fact, more than that, an organiser of others."

"I expect that's because we've known him for a while," Paul replied, "and because he's come to church fairly regularly."

"I wonder why — he's come to church, I mean!"

"It was probably just a front — a front of respectability to cover his activities. He must often have felt uncomfortable under the preaching."

"Oh, shut up, you two!" David exclaimed irritably.

Paul grinned. "We just want him to know what we think of him If he's listening," he said. "Anyway, it could be a lot worse, couldn't it? At least we now know whom we are up against. In fact, we know so much he could easily have shot us all," he ended cheerfully.

David gave an exaggerated sigh and reminded his

brother that they were not out of the place yet.

"We might know more than we did," Alan remarked, "but he didn't tell us why he sent Tony Masterson to us — or whatever his name is. That doesn't make sense."

"It's no use trying to work things out," David retorted. "We are always wrong."

"I liked Tony, that night," Paul said, "and I am far more disappointed in him than in Dr. Mason. Dr. Mason never pretended to be a christian, but he did, and he seemed just like one — you can usually tell, can't you?"

"It was his halo that did it," David said sarcastically.

To his surprise, his two companions saw the funny side of his remark and began to discuss the merits of their own imaginary halos with the aid of the mirror above the old fireplace. This frivolous interlude broke the tension and, apart from anxiety about Liz, would almost have relaxed, resigned to let matters take their own course.

Dr. Mason himself returned with coffee and sandwiches. "Sorry if the coffee is a bit strong," he apologised. "Joe obviously prefers to eat it." No-one laughed and he paused as he walked back to the door. "Don't be too critical of me, David. Like me, you are of an independent turn of mind. Don't be restricted into a mould. Be yourself. What does it matter if your philosophy isn't exactly that of your neighbour? Who is to say which is the right one? If more things are legitimate to me, from my particular viewpoint, than most people would allow, I can still have a 'god' of my own."

"You have no God in heaven. You have made a god of your money and of yourself," David said, turning away.

As Dr. Mason left without another word, his captors turned silently to the food he had brought. In spite of their preoccupation, the sight of it made them eager to eat, and the steaming cups of coffee would help to warm them up, for it was cold in the big room without a fire. They dreaded to imagine how Liz was feeling outside and wished they could take one of the cups out to her.

The coffee was certainly too strong for their liking but the sandwiches tasted marvellous with their thick ham and pickles. For a while they ate in silence.

"How long do you think they'll keep us here, David?" Alan asked eventually, thinking of their parents.

"Who can tell?" David replied. "Long enough to give them time to disappear at least. That could mean hours or it could mean days. If only I'd told you to ring home instead of Dr. Mason! We might have been home again now," he groaned, feeling the full weight of responsibility as the eldest.

"It's no use thinking of what might have been," Alan replied sensibly, finishing the last sandwich and draining his cup. "The question is whether or not there is anything we can do as circumstances are."

"I find it difficult thinking of anything," David replied, putting his hand to his head. "Either the strain or the cold is affecting me."

"I'm sleepy," Paul said, "but I'm also still hungry. I could eat those sandwiches all over again."

Their comments became fewer. It became too much effort to speak.

Alan made a determined effort. "That letter must have incriminated Dr. Mason pretty badly," he commented in a somewhat unnatural voice. "Did you . . . did you read . . . ?" He tried to concentrate on what he was saying. There had been a letter behind a picture — *that* picture, but how could it be floating away as it was? "David, I do feel queer."

But David did not seem to hear him. His head was rolling and his eyes trying to focus on the articles on the table before him.

Paul jumped to his feet, knocking a plate to the floor as he did so. On his feet, he staggered and sat down again, clutching at the edge of the table. He stared down at three empty mugs and groaned. "They've . . . got . . . us . . . again," he drawled. "We've . . . ," but he couldn't get out the rest of the sentence, furnishing the others with the unnecessary information that they had been drugged.

Chapter 15

As Alan and Dr. Mason went indoors, Liz told herself that their ordeal was almost over. Why then that sixth sense warning her to be extra careful since she was now on her own? Unaccountable as the instinct might be, she heeded it, staying quietly in the black as night centre of the old yew. She wondered why it was she had not gone with Alan to join Dr. Mason. His car standing conspicuously in front of the house suggested that Dr. Mason planned an open confrontation, but how could one man command any authority over one or more lawless ones? Was that what held her back — the fear of his being taken captive, too? She shook her head in bewilderment. Why come himself instead of sending the police? But most likely it was not *instead* of, but *as well* as. They would come any minute. Then they would all be safe again and life would gradually become normal.

Liz allowed herself to visualise their final victory. The men would be led away handcuffed, the incriminating document would — hopefully — be handed over to the authorities and Christopher would be immediately released. That would partly atone for the anxiety their parents must be experiencing on their behalf even now, despite the fact that help was on the way.

The moon went behind a big bank of cloud, giving her the opportunity of moving forward so she could watch the house more closely. Not that there was much to see. There was an uncanny lack of activity or noise. Why did Dr. Mason and the boys not come out? She had expected them to be only a few minutes. Why did nothing happen as they expected?

Dare she return to the window of the room Paul had climbed into, now that it was dark? In all probability the curtains would now be drawn but she might possibly hear something. It was worth going to see. Like a shadow she crept back to the road and along it until she reached the gable end window. It was closed and covered.

Only a tiny gap at one bottom corner revealed a fragmentary portion of the room too small to be of any use. There was a drone of muffled voices, but her straining ears could not pick out a single word. It was not worth her standing there any longer, risking exposure out in the open. It was best to get back to the yew tree where she could see without being seen.

She had just settled herself again in her aromatic hiding place, thinking gratefully that the evening was definitely warmer now, when another car approached, its headlights giving her warning a full minute before its actual arrival. Hope sprang again to Liz's heart but died once more when she observed that it was not a police car any more than the last two had been. Tony Masterson! She had forgotten his intention of coming here during the evening. Her heart thumped wildly. What would happen now? She could think of nothing, nothing at all to do to intervene. The man hardly glanced at the doctor's car but went straight indoors, leaving Liz in a frenzy of panic. She beat her forehead with her hands without realising she was doing it, trying to decide what to do. If the occupants of the house didn't know of Dr. Mason's presence, they would find out as soon as Tony Masterson mentioned his car outside. He hadn't a chance of getting away with the boys.

Liz groaned. She would have to go and seek another house with a telephone, after all. That might take time, but it was all that she could do. However, she still lingered, for fear of the house being shut up and everyone disappeared when she returned.

After ten minutes, when she was about to move, Tony Masterson appeared again, a torch in his hand. He walked casually past Dr. Mason's car and made for the deepest shadows. He was clearly searching, his torch probing every dark place among the bushes, in the angles of the walls and anywhere else where something or someone could lay concealed. Either they had got Dr. Mason and were wanting to be sure he had brought no-one with him, or one of the boys had betrayed her presence with them and they were seeking her. She remained where she was, but wondered if she could dodge round to ground the man had already covered. It would be too risky. Hastily she felt around to see if she could strengthen her position. If Tony came here and flashed his light in her direction, all would be over. A steeply sloping branch rose from the ground behind her. If it was strong enough to bear her weight she would try to get more into the thick foliage. Half climbing and half pulling herself up with her hands she rose slowly above ground level, slowly so that she made no noise to give her presence away and slowly so that she did not hit her head on the tangle of branches above. The foliage was so thick that she was completely enmeshed and badly scratched, but she did not care as long as she was hidden.

Joe sauntered over to Tony Masterson with a second torch.

"There's no-one here. The boss must be wrong," Tony said, coming near Liz's hiding place. The boss — here! Liz's heart sank.

"What's it matter?" Joe grumbled. "We'd be away before she'd time to bring help, anyway."

A rough branch end was poking very uncomfortably into the bottom of Liz's back but she clung there, hardly daring to breathe. The pungent smell of yew was strong in her nostrils and she felt she would never smell it again without a shudder. The rays of light were alarmingly close to her feet, illuminating the place she had so recently vacated at the base of the tree. She closed her eyes, not able to bear to watch the sweeping beams of light. She could not close her ears, though, and she expected to hear their accusing voices addressing her at any minute. At last she dared to open her eyes again. The lights were moving away. Carefully she dropped to the ground, trusting that they would not return. They had made it clear they were not expecting to find anyone. Anyway, it was much too uncomfortable in the branches to remain there indefinitely, and her view of the house had been completely obliterated.

She dare not leave the grounds after what she had heard, though she did not know what to do if she stayed. If only they had known that the man behind these criminals was here already, they might have been more careful not to walk, one by one, straight into his clutches! She had no doubt now but that Dr. Mason was being forcibly detained with the others. What else could explain their non-appearance?

Liz sat down on the old, dry foliage on the floor of her hiding place, leaning back on the branch she had climbed. There had been so many alarms and disappointments that a reaction began to set in. Her mind seemed to be going numb like her legs, refusing to keep a tangible hold on reality.

"I shouldn't have sat down. I must get up again," she told herself, but she didn't. She must stay alert and keep watch, but she found herself unable to do that, either. Her physical constitution was at last rebelling and she found herself half asleep. She reclined in that condition, sometimes insensible and sometimes returning to vague consciousness until she suddenly came completely back to reality with a start. The slamming of a car door had roused her. It was the passenger door of Dr. Mason's car. On the seat Liz could see a form with fair hair gleaming under the car's interior light. She realised with a shock that it looked like Alan. The other three doors were wide open.

Liz gasped. A man came out carrying what looked like the dead body of Paul and she shuddered with the horror of it, almost screaming out involuntarily. Even at this distance she could see the familiar comic still sticking out of the top of his pocket. Paul, dear, funny Paul! What had she done to them all? She grasped the branch near her hand to stop herself rushing out to an impossible rescue, and she told herself that Paul was unconscious, not dead. This seemed to be proved by the fact that David came next in line, still on his feet, but half pushed and half carried by Joe and Tony Masterson.

Only then did she notice who carried Paul, and the sight brought the blood rushing to her face. It was Dr. Mason himself, and he was so obviously with the men and not against them! She thought at first that the men must be forcing him to help them, but it was clearly not so. Liz's shock was so great that she found difficulty in grasping the truth, but was eventually forced to draw the inevitable conclusion that they had been tricked and betrayed by a very clever but contemptible man. Liz shook with fury, with dismay and with frustration, for the moment hating Dr. Mason for what he'd done to them and blaming herself unreasonably for not tumbling to the truth sooner.

Afterwards, Liz always maintained that God spoke to her in that moment by a star more clearly than He could have with an audible voice, and His message was one of rebuke and comfort at one and the same time, for the clouds parted, revealing a twinkling heavenly body in a clear patch of sky. She had forgotten that He was there, that He was all seeing and all powerful. The star was a timely reminder that for the whole of time God would continue to maintain His ordered universe and work all things together for the good of those who belonged to Him. With a grateful sigh and without conscious effort she pulled herself together, remembering that hatred and the desire for revenge must have no part in her as a christian and that she must guard carefully against impulsive action if she was going to pit her wits against this man.

In spite of herself, Liz could not help but feel an admiration for the part Dr. Mason had played. A part it was, and he had not given them a single hint of the man he really was. They had never doubted it was out of concern for them he had as good as warned them not to get involved. Oh, yes, he was a top class actor, and the real life person was not the one they had hitherto known. They had known him in his role, the role of genial, church going, law abiding citizen!

As the boys were bundled with a certain amount of difficulty into the car, Liz caught the occasional word from Dr. Mason and the men.

"Carefully . . . not safe here . . . not sure how much they know . . . warehouse . . . tomorrow lunch time . . . abroad." All of which told Liz nothing definite.

The men closed the doors and ran back into the house.

Liz had to decide what to do, and decide quickly. There could be no wavering this time. She ran to one of the solitary trees between shrubbery and house and paused, concealed behind it. She had no idea where they were going and she needed to know, if she were going to do anything to help. Quickly, she made her decision. It had to be action of one kind or another. Determined to keep close to the others, she proceeded to do the only thing she could think of. The house lights were going off one by one. She had no time to lose. Leaving her hiding place, she ran to Dr. Mason's car and tried the boot. It opened at her touch and was empty. She lifted the cover and scrambled inside, curled herself into a ball and pulled it down after her. If Dr. Mason decided to put something into the boot, that was just too bad! However, she was left undisturbed and she felt the driver get in almost immediately. The door slammed and the car vibrated as the engine started up. She was just in time.

From the first crunch of gravel under the tyres, it was a nightmare journey for Liz. Dr. Mason drove at a breakneck speed, uncharacteristic of Liz's old image of him, and the stowaway in his boot was sent sliding first one way and then the other as he hardly slowed down for bends or hills. Her primary concern was not to let go of the lid of the boot, but she was sure she couldn't keep hold of it if he were going far. The movement didn't feel like forward motion at all, but as if she were being spun in a washing machine.

Her only immediate companion was a can of petrol, the smell of which was even more overpowering than the yew foliage had been. It made her feel sick and the motion made her dizzy. Would this nightmare never end, this nightmare which hadn't just started with the present journey, but all those endless weeks ago on the evening when Christopher had met the real Tony? As in all nightmares, the characters were caught up in a chain of events that were gradually accumulating up to that one inevitable moment of horror prior to waking. If only she *could* wake up and find she had been dreaming!

Dr. Mason swerved suddenly and Liz was again thrown slithering to the other end of the smelly boot. He must have been passing another vehicle, for immediately afterwards there was a powerful light behind them and Liz feared they would notice the unsecured boot and her fingers sticking out. The other car was not in as great a hurry as Dr. Mason, however, and the lights fell back and soon all was dark again. Later, she heard a train nearby, and not long after that the ground became bumpy and uneven, making the strain on her fingers almost unendurable. The final jolt was the worst, and she involuntarily cried out in pain as the car, without warning, shuddered to a standstill, pulling dreadfully at the boot cover then suddenly trapping her fingers with a snap between the two pieces of metal. With stars before her eyes and fighting the spasmodic tendency to pass out, Liz was dimly conscious of car doors opening and closing again, and of voices close by.

As the ache in her fingers became less excruciating, Liz realised she must take stock of her new surroundings, and peeped cautiously out. She noticed with surprise that they were no longer out in bleak country but in a dark, cobbled yard surrounded by what appeared to be old warehouses. The windows in the nearest building were mostly broken. Immediately beside the car was an untidy stack of rusty metal drums. The whole yard was extremely dark except for where the light from the main doorway fell, and Liz felt safe to look around more closely. The voices moved further away and as she lifted the boot cover a bit more, she saw Dr. Mason and a stranger dragging David inside that one central door between them. She glanced carefully down one side of the car and then the other, but no-one was there. As soon as the men were out of sight, Liz tumbled out of her hiding place as quickly as she could, hoping to be able to hide behind the stack of drums. This proved rather difficult because, slim though she was, there was scarcely any room between them and the wall. However, she had the advantage of darkness, and she knew she could not afford to stay there for long. She must get inside the building and, somehow, she must *act*. She was the only person who could do anything now towards their cause, so it was her responsibility to do so. With renewed purpose, she determined she would win this contest yet and, if not, she would at least go down fighting to her last breath.

The younger boys were still absolutely limp and unconscious. Dr. Mason and his companion carried one each in their arms into the building. Liz followed them at what she hoped would be a safe distance. Inside the door, she found herself in a completely empty room, empty that is except for an incredible accumulation of cobwebs and dirt. This was no building in current commercial use, nor had been for a long time. At the far end, a door led into a long passage. Liz moved noiselessly along this, following the voices and the heavy, fresh footprints in the dust of the floor, then up a steep flight of steps and along another corridor. The voices were just in front now, and Liz stopped short at a bend in the passage after only one glimpse of an open door from which the light streamed out. The room terminated the passage, its door facing the stairs along its length. It was apparently the room where the boys were being imprisoned.

Liz stepped back into a shadowy doorway but the light from in front still penetrated enough to betray her presence. She heard a key being turned in a lock and knew that the men were going again. She tried the door behind her and it opened easily, so she slipped into the concealing darkness beyond. Instinctively she moved behind the door as she silently closed it again. In the pitch darkness she groped around until she found the wall. Then her hands felt material hanging there. It had a sticky, dirty touch and smelled musty and she knew it had been there for a long while. She shuddered with repulsion, hating the staleness of the place. The next moment she was full of thankfulness for those hanging draperies, filthy though they were, for someone had obviously grasped the door knob of the room she was in. Without a second's hesitation she dived between the wall and them. The dust and smell nauseated her but, gratefully, she realised that she was covered, at least down to her ankles. She just had time, too, to be glad that she was unable to see any cobwebs there might be — not to mention their inhabitants — before a light was switched on and she could see a textured glow through the old warehouse coats behind which she hid. There was no time to reproach herself for coming in here. Rather, she must seek to take advantage of her position. If only she could be sure her feet were not showing!

"They'll be out for an hour or two yet." Both Dr. Mason and his companion were in the room. "They won't feel too good when they do come round, so I don't think you'll have any trouble with them."

The other man grunted. "I don't know why you had to bring them here at all," he grumbled. "They were alright for a night at Crow End, without all this panic."

"I tell you, they knew too much. How, I haven't the faintest notion, but if they knew of that letter I was foolish enough to write, and if they knew about Crow End, in all probability others knew of those details, too — almost certainly Elizabeth Meyer, whose absence from the others I can't understand, quite frankly. We can't afford their being traced until tomorrow lunch time at the earliest. I begin to wish we'd never touched the Hampshire diamonds. The job was jinxed from the very beginning with that confounded cat," Dr. Mason observed superstitiously.

"I fail to see why that cat made you as jittery as it did," the other replied dryly. "The whole outcome was cut and dried in our favour. All that panic as to whether their key witness would turn up! — What difference did it make? It was too late to matter."

Dr. Mason was hardly Liz's favourite character at the moment, but this man even less so, with the scathing inflections in his voice. The doctor seemed not to notice.

"It was safer that investigations were not reopened until we'd wound up our business affairs. There's no telling what would have come to light. Even now I suspect other investigations being conducted which are rather too close for comfort."

"Those kids can't trouble us now, anyway."

"Silly little fools," Dr. Mason muttered reflectively. "Pity they insisted in getting mixed up in it all. I'd rather they'd been able to go on thinking of me as . . . " Liz heard the shrug in his voice.

His companion apparently felt no sentiment at all. "Pity for *them?*" he asked incredulously. "What about us? In danger of a complete showdown, biggest job planned having to be abandoned, having to clear out in undignified haste, leaving things behind we would otherwise have disposed of, and financially . . . "

"You have no cause for complaint as far as I can see," Dr. Mason replied in deceptively silky tones. "You will have all your dues shortly with little trouble and no risk in earning it. There's nothing to lead anyone here, and no-one will come back on you afterwards. Your prisoners do not know you, and this derelict and forsaken building is only being 'borrowed' by you for a short time. Now Masterson, Joe and I are in a different position. The game is up for us. If we stay put, we can be dug out quite easily with all that our friends in there know about us. As detection is inevitable, all we can do is detain those who would 'inform' on us until we can be safely out

214

of their reach. They have little on Lenny, and he is going to take the risk of being picked up. But you, my friend, can relax safely.'' The doctor's voice was ominously quiet and edged with contempt.

''There's no guarantee you won't inform . . . '' the man muttered.

''You forget I won't be here to inform.'' Dr. Mason was angry now, his tones sharp and clipped. ''Besides, I don't work like that. My activities might be regarded as suspect by the law of the land, and myself therefore as a transgressor of that law, but there is a point where I draw the line, and 'informing' would come under that heading.''

Liz fumed within herself. ''Words!'' she thought. He mightn't exactly have 'informed' against Christopher, but he hadn't drawn the line at his having to pay for the doctor's crimes!

''Here's the key,'' Dr. Mason continued coldly, and there was no sound to betray to Liz what the man had done with it. ''Help me to get this pile of stuff in the boot, then I'll be off.''

When Liz heard them both go down the stairs, she poked her head out, taking deep breaths of relatively clean air. Her nose and throat felt full of choking dust. She stayed where she was, however. She had a good hiding place and she had a job to do which meant keeping in close proximity with the boys' jailor. She had to get that key — somehow — and let them out of their prison. She did, however, risk taking a step forward to reach the drawer handle of an old desk to make sure the man had not put the key in there. There was only one thing in the drawer — a revolver. Liz closed the drawer again with a shudder, and retreated behind her screen.

She looked round the room. The only other furniture' in it was an uncomfortable looking wooden chair. There was a pile of boxes on the desk that Liz guessed were on their way into Dr. Mason's boot.

"I hope they are more comfortable than I was," she thought mirthlessly.

Liz saw that there had never been any danger that her feet would be noticed as there were piles of ancient rubbish on the floor at her side of the room which extended in front of the coats, boxes, screwed up paper and bits of old rag. The floorboards were covered with thick dust and, to Liz's concern, she noticed that the step she had taken forward was clearly imprinted in it. She did all she could think of and threw one of the dusty rags over it. Next she looked closer at her hiding place, then wished she hadn't! In all the folds of the garments cobwebs had formed over the years and Liz felt she couldn't go behind again. But when she heard the men returning, she closed her eyes and forced herself to do so. A shiver went down her spine as she imagined she felt spiders in her hair.

"I can manage these last few boxes," Dr. Mason informed his companion abruptly. "You stay here. I want no slip up this time, remember. I'll be back at noon tomorrow to pick up Joe and Masterson who should get here a bit earlier in a van borrowed for the purpose. We will just be in time for the plane at half past one. In the meantime, I've plenty of loose ends to be tying up."

The door closed quietly and single footsteps grew fainter. The man must have stood without moving for five minutes and Liz sensed he was angry. Dr. Mason's tone of voice? Or was it that he was having to wait until the very last minute for those 'dues' he had been promised? More likely, he simply resented the job he'd been given.

At last the man muttered something Liz could not catch and began to move around the room. Surely he would not come to her corner! No-one had touched these coats for years.

Liz wished she had looked at her watch when she'd had the chance. It must be nearly night. Presumably the man would sleep when he considered it to be time. That was her most likely chance to get hold of that key. She must work carefully. There were still a lot of hours at her disposal, and if she made no mistakes there was yet time to bring these men to a just retribution for all their misdeeds.

Chapter 16

David's first thought on awaking was that his bed had suddenly become very uncomfortable. It had developed bony ridges and felt hard all over. Then his head and a strong wave of nausea reminded him that he was at Crow End, an isolated farmhouse seemingly a thousand miles and a thousand decades from home. His spirits, in his boots yesterday, sank below the floorboards now. They were at the mercy of ruthless men who had outwitted them from the beginning. It afforded little consolation to him that he was still alive, for they remained in the hands of ruffians who could yet do anything. It was still dark and David could see nothing of his surroundings. The silence suddenly shocked him. He had been thinking in the plural, but perhaps even now he was alone, the only one alive. It had been poison and not a sleeping draught they'd been given. He shook himself, unaware of the sobbing breath he had taken, asking himself why he was not dead too, in that case.

"David, are you awake?" It was Paul's voice and was close beside him.

David's relief was immense. "Just. Not exactly a five star hotel, is it?"

"I've been awake a while," his brother replied, "and have already come to certain conclusions, so I'll tell you in order to save you the effort of having to work them out for yourself. If your head's as reluctant to work as mine was to start with . . ." He did not finish the sentence.

"All I want to know is the way out."

"That I can't tell you," Paul replied. ". . . Usually through a door, but the door is locked, needless to say. I've tried it. And in the rather difficult process of finding it, I also discovered that we are not in the same room as we went to sleep in. The first thing I did was put my hand out and touch bare boards — no carpet. In fact, no *anything* but us and our hastily made beds of old rags and newspaper. Alan is on the other side of me, still asleep. Before I got back in my feather bed I peered through the window but couldn't see a thing. However, I didn't need to see anything to tell me that we are not even in the same building as last night!"

"What!"

"If you think back to Crow End, you will recall that intermittently we were serenaded by mournful sheep. There has been no evidence of sheep here. At Crow End there was no traffic to call anything, and it was gravel underfoot. There is plenty of traffic some distance away from here, some of it heavy and, what's more, the occasional vehicle immediately outside sounds to be going over cobbles. The final proof was the ships."

"Ships!"

"We must be near a shipyard or harbour. I'm sure they are ships' hooters I keep hearing."

"Oh, my head! I wish I could think. I wonder where . . . " David stopped. He was going to add, "where Elizabeth is," then remembered in time that someone might be listening, either inside the room or out. "Let's leave it until daylight, shall we, there's a good lad. You never know what crooks are listening," he added in a loud voice as if to challenge any unseen eavesdropper. But there was no reply and he sighed in irritation.

In the distance a siren sounded. Yes, it was a ship's hooter, David decided. The coast must be near, but which coast? Perhaps they were going to be taken abroad. David felt so ill and emotionally spent that the thought brought no feeling with it and, not surprisingly, he was asleep again before long. Paul, listening to the regular, heavy breathing, wished the light would come. Then at least he could read his comic which he had felt with satisfaction to be still in his pocket. He screwed up his eyes and peered into the darkness, probing like a blind man with his stick. There was a single infinitesimally less dark oblong that was the window, but not even a star through it.

Paul got up again. The padding beneath him felt damp and he was cold. He was still unsteady with the effects of the drug, but a bit more movement might warm him up. He forced himself across to the lighter patch and back again where he staggered over a recumbent figure on the floor. He heard the gasp of a sleeper suddenly awakened, and expected to hear an angry exclamation from his brother. But he was amazed, after a certain amount of shifting and disentangling, to hear a different but vaguely familiar voice speaking comfortingly.

"Go back to sleep, boy. It's only half past three."

Paul saw the flash of a luminous dial.

"Who . . . ?"

"In the morning," was the quiet rejoinder. "You're alright here, but there's nothing you can do. Might as well sleep."

So Paul groped his way from the mystery man to David and from David to his own empty and not very inviting couch. Instead of lying on top, he bored his way into the middle of the untidy heap and, surprisingly, fell asleep before he had time to ponder over the identity of the stranger in their midst.

But sleep had gone for the latter and he sat up, leaning against the wall. He was still sitting in the same position when David woke again in the grey of dawn and caught his eye. He saw the surprised start and the setting of his lips.

"Honoured, I'm sure," David muttered sarcastically. "Fancy having Tony Masterson for our jailor!

221

Now we can tell you what we think of you."

The face of the older man was impassive. In the long preceding hours he had been wondering what the reaction of the youngsters would be to his presence.

"I think I'd better explain something first."

"There is certainly a lot for you to start on," David said dryly. "But for you we wouldn't be in this position."

"I'm in exactly the same position as you, except that I've been here rather longer. The key is turned on me as well as you."

"A likely tale! We know all about where you were yesterday."

"As I said before, there is something you should know." He glanced at the still sleeping figures of Alan and Paul. "I was intending telling you all together but there is no point in waking them, so it seems I'll have to explain twice."

"Well?" David said, waiting. "There's absolutely nothing you could say to condone your treatment of us."

"Sorry to prove you wrong," the other replied gently. "The thing you do not know, but need to know, is that I have a twin brother."

David had imagined himself beyond surprises by then but this one stunned him. He knew instinctively that it was true, and he felt a fool. The others had been right. The first Tony had been genuine enough. Except in appearance, there was no resemblance between the two men. Their bearing and personalities were poles apart. Alan had said they were like two different men. He had hit the nail on the head without knowing it. The picture was becoming clearer.

"Then . . . then the only time we've met you was the night at my home?"

"Quite true. I've been here since late that night," Tony nodded. "vainly fuming because I could not warn you any more than I could help you."

"What happened . . . when you left us?"

"Two fellows met me down the road, one they call 'Boss' and a swarthy individual with a moustache."

"Dr. Mason and Lenny," David deduced, bitterness again welling up inside him against his old idol.

"They were waiting for me," Tony Masterson continued, "with the intention of bribing me to silence until a more 'convenient' time for them. I admit their generosity staggered me! When I would not bite, they hustled me at gunpoint into a car standing in the shadows. I told you when I left that my brother was waiting for me — it might have saved a lot of trouble if I'd said he was an identical twin — and he was in the car by that time, having already been 'bought', all ready to offer his services in return for the intoxicating amount of money he'd been promised if I would not co-operate. They were not slow to see his value as the one able to give the lie to your story."

"So they forced you to do a disappearing act and

he was sent to your house to deny everything if the police came seeking him — you, I mean."

"Right again. Then apparently you met up with 'me' again . . . "

"It's all so clear now! That's why he hardly seemed to recognise us the day we accosted him on the street — he *didn't* recognise us for he'd never seen us before! How blind we were — in more ways than one!"

"So I was one of the ogres to you all?" It was a question rather than a statement, quietly spoken but with a note of reproof.

David flushed. "The others were less inclined to see you in that light in those early stages," he admitted, "and I apologise. They defended you until the evidence against seemed conclusive. But I believe you now."

Tony Masterson studied him meditatively, then he smiled and held out his hand, aware of David's embarrassment. "Shake on it," he said brightly, "then tell me what has happened to you all, because the information I've managed to glean is very meagre."

Gratefully, David launched into an account of their activities. It took a great deal of telling, but Tony listened attentively. To his credit, David did not spare himself in the account. "So you see," he concluded, "we've been well and truly duped all along the line, and we're more helpless now than ever. What can we do stuck here?"

"A lot."

"What do you mean?"

"I've been praying ever since I woke up at three thirty and prayer opens more doors than we ever could — or at least the One we pray to does."

"It hasn't opened *this* door, the one that matters!" David's old scepticism showed itself again.

"That's a silly remark, David," Tony Masterson replied bluntly. "I didn't say I was praying to a fairy godmother to wave a magic wand, or to a Father Christmas to give me just what I want. It's God's will we've to seek in all this, His purposes we have to fathom, and His lessons we have to learn. One of the first texts Christopher quoted to me was, "In all thy ways acknowledge Him and He shall direct thy paths'. But you've never 'acknowledged' Him, have you, David!"

"I haven't asked for my sins to be forgiven as if I were a murderer or something, nor to be saved from hell," David replied employing the religious terminology of which he was so critical. "I don't believe in hell, anyway. I can't imagine how anyone can believe in hell and stay sane."

Without a moment's hesitation Tony turned the tables on him. "You might say the same thing about death," he said, "but only a fool would say they didn't believe in it. You're burying your head in the sand as I was, refusing to face the truth."

"I'm not intentionally doing that — I don't think," David replied more carefully. "Basically, I suppose it's the credibility of christianity I find difficulty with. I'd rather trust in facts than

225

suppositions. There is evidence to my eyes as to the reality of things around me. Scientific theories can be tested and proved or disproved, and mathematics are definite. It seems foolish to put one's faith in things that can't be proved."

"I could dispute the claims you make for science," Tony replied with a slight smile, "but never mind! As you have no doubt studied them to some degree, I assume you have equally considered the evidences on the side of christianity — for evidences there are, make no mistake. As a lecturer in Comparative Religions, I knew that. The witness of secular history to such facts as the crucifiction and resurrection, fulfilled prophesies concerning individuals and nations after hundreds of years, being but two examples. Add to these objective considerations the subjective testimony of changed lives and the evidence is considerable. But I suspect," he added shrewdly, "that you have come to your conclusions a little hastily."

David had the grace to look shamefaced, yet he had not ceased to struggle for his theories. "Most intellectual people don't think as you do," he objected.

"The proof of a thing is not in the number of its adherents as many a scientist has found out when presenting new discoveries. The Bible makes it clear that christians would always be in the minority and it also gives the explanation, the blinding of men's eyes by the devil, in order to make a mess of their lives."

226

"And then there's a danger of turning to religion just to get you out of a mess," David argued. "Mightn't that be why you . . . ? As an escape from trouble?"

"If I'd become a christian earlier, I wouldn't have got into trouble to the same extent! But it seems I needed it to convince me of my need of salvation. Perhaps your ordeal is for the same purpose, David."

David fell silent. He had met more than his match in Tony Masterson. He chided himself for his inability mentally to compete with him and for the first time he saw his intellectual aspirations as the mere cover up they had been.

As if reading his mind, the other man continued earnestly, "Intellect is in the same category as wealth and position, David, a snare rather than a benefit if not subject to God. I had all three, more money than I could use, a university status, at the forefront of contemporary thought, but I was as depressed and miserable as if I'd had none of them. They did not prevent my breakdown. I will not explain how everything came to a head. The fact is that man is soul as well as body and that night in Christopher's flat God stepped into my life and made me spiritually alive. What about Dr. Mason? What did his intellect do for him except to make him a clever criminal? With only his kind in the world, it would be a perilous place."

Mention of Dr. Mason broke down the remainder of David's resistence and he knew he had to face the issues. "I need to think," he exclaimed, springing up so suddenly that Alan and Paul woke with a start. He went over to the window and stared out, hardly conscious of the exclamations and conversation behind him or the scene through the glass in front.

All the time Tony was patiently talking with Alan and Paul, his sympathies were with David standing dejectedly at the window. All told, David had more than them all to gain or lose from their ordeals, and Tony prayed it would all be gain. But David had to live his own life and could only agonise for himself. Tony had pointed the way. However, his own spiritual struggles were so recent that he could not help but identify and sympathise with him.

David was still standing there when the boys came over to join him.

"Anything worth seeing?" Paul enquired in cheerful form.

Though he had been staring out, the scene had not registered on David until now.

"A cobbled yard, dilapidated buildings — and rain," David smiled.

"It *is* rather grotty, isn't it?" his brother agreed, but they peered out to see what their situation offered.

What it offered was precious little. They were three floors up the warehouse front and there was no-one in sight below. The whole scene suggested decay and abandonment. David looked with distaste at the oily patches in the pools on the cobbles. His eyes suddenly went to a moving object which had come into their line of vision, a large, graceful, gliding seagull, its whiteness strangely incongruous against its sombre backcloth.

"Oh, God," David prayed silently but earnestly, his heart moved, "make my proud, sinful heart as white as that bird in such a scene of grime." To his surprise, a great sense of relief flooded him and he impulsively ruffled Paul's hair in affection. It was Paul's turn to be surprised.

"What's up? Have you seen something?" his brother asked, glancing back to the yard below.

"Yes, I've seen something," David acknowledged emphatically. "Not out there, though. In my mind. I'll explain later." A glance at the faces around him showed that only one of his companions understood his words and he was glad of Tony Masterson's warm smile. "But for the moment we'd better put our heads together to think of something that will get us out of here."

Chapter 17

Pastor Meyer began to wonder whether he ought to have taken the doctor's advice and snatched a quick break. He felt tired that Saturday morning and his wife, unusually, had admitted that she was, too. Not only did they have the pastoral responsibility for a busy church, but recent events had taken more out of them than they at first realised. She particularly felt grateful not to have been involved in all the youngsters' activities of this last week. That which might have been the final straw to her resistance had proved to be good for the young people, transforming them almost overnight from teenagers to adults. They had learned to come to terms with disappointment, to take the initiative and to face responsibilities. Liz was still impetuous, but no doubt she would always be, to some degree!

Pastor Meyer came out of his study half way through the morning, a piece of paper containing Tony Masterson's address in his hand.

"Have they gone into Town?" he asked. "I could have given them a lift but I've only just decided to go. There was no concentrating on what I was doing, so I've decided to go and have a further word with the police."

"They went early," his wife replied, "and I don't think it will be long before they're back." Her eyes followed him to the door. "Dinner will be about one o'clock, a special one in honour of Liz's birthday. She'll have more time to appreciate it than last night. I think I'll ring the Ransoms to see if its alright for David and Paul to stay."

She dismissed the thought of her husband's mission from her mind as a precaution against false hopes and concentrated on more mundane things, whether or not she had put the salt in the vegetables and which pudding to make. To her surprise, the pastor was the first of her family to return and he was hurrying, conscious that he was late.

"I was afraid I'd be holding things up," he apologised. "Not back yet?"

"No. The dinner's going to spoil if they don't come soon. They are usually back by this time. I should have told them not to be late — but they're always here for lunch."

"They'll be here any minute."

She nodded. "How did you get on?"

"The sergeant down there is very sympathetic, you know, Jill. I feel quite encouraged after a chat with him. Apparently there has been some renewed discussion about the Hampshire case since Liz and

231

David called in about Tony Masterson. Further enquiries have been made and they are far from satisfied with their findings — I don't exactly know the details."

Mrs. Meyer glanced for the dozenth time down the empty garden path, then began to put steaming dishes into the hot oven. "Dissatisfied? Why?"

"Well, apparently Masterson has been acting strangely this week, avoiding contact with his neighbours, setting off each morning but not turning up at his work. He sent his employers a notification of sickness but hasn't seen his doctor. In spite of several attempts, the police have not managed to contact him again since the day he denied any knowledge of that advertisement."

"Has he not got a wife?"

"She died a short while ago in a road accident. They had no children. The only other relative the police know of is a brother, but they've not managed to find him, either."

"But there are no other new developments?"

"Not directly concerning our case, but they seem to have some fresh light on one of the related cases, the Newton Gallery theft, I believe they said. If the two affairs *are* connected, it might help us indirectly."

"Oh, Martin! I'm glad I'm a housewife and a pastor's wife, rather than a policeman's. What complicated tangles they have to work out!"

He laughed. "Your job isn't without its difficulties," he replied, "when lunch is ready and every one of the family late for it! That camera must be presenting a problem."

"I thought she had chosen one and that they only had to get it."

After waiting another ten minutes, they decided to eat. They talked while they ate, puzzled rather than worried. However, Jill did voice her hopes that they were not walking into trouble on Christopher's behalf.

"Don't worry," Pastor Meyer consoled her. "David wouldn't do that. Anyway, I don't see what more they could do." He paused, thoughtful. "Actually, I have been wondering whether I should call on Lester Addison — the chap Christopher worked with. You remember Liz telling us about the peculiar incident David witnessed in that cafe."

"Oh, you can't, Martin! It would be like accusing . . ."

"I know it's probably irrelevant," he said, "but it was a puzzling incident and Addison *had* been in close contact with the diamonds until the very day of their disappearance. I debated whether to mention the incident to the sergeant this morning but didn't want to cause trouble for the lad if there was a simple explanation. He'd probably resent my going to him, as Christopher's father, but that can't be helped. I think I'll see if I can find him this afternoon. If he's in the shop, Mr. Raynor will let us talk in the back. Don't worry, I'll be tactful. I don't want to get in trouble for making false accusations."

Left on her own again, Mrs. Meyer began to feel

annoyed that her family could have been so thoughtless as to stay away so long without a phone call to explain. Liz and Alan weren't usually inconsiderate, though, so she made an attempt to defer any annoyance at their absence until she knew the reason why.

The telephone rang. It was Mrs. Ransom anxious to discuss certain church matters. The two were close friends and they talked on after the main topic of conversation had been exhausted.

"Those youngsters haven't returned there, by any chance?" Jill Meyer asked eventually.

"No." She could hear the surprise at the other end of the line. "I assumed they'd lunched with you and stayed on."

"We haven't seen them yet."

"But it will soon be teatime! Where can they be?"

"They'll be alright," Jill replied. "There are four of them. No doubt there will be some simple explanation."

"There's no telling, these days," her friend snorted cynically.

Jill laughed in spite of her growing anxiety, then heard the manse door. "Someone has come in," she said. "It's probably them — no, sorry, it's Martin. Anyway, the first one of us to see them can let the other know."

She shook her head in answer to her husband's query. He had not seen them, nor had he seen Lester Addiston, whom John Raynor had sent out on firm's business.

It was barely ten minutes later, however, that the doorbell rang and, to Pastor Meyer's surprise, Lester Addison was admitted by his wife. They were struck immediately by his extreme nervousness. The kettle was boiling, so Jill made a mug of coffee which she placed on the kitchen table in front of the redhead, but his hands dithered when he picked it up. They did their best to put him at his ease but he did not seem to be able to relax or to speak.

"It's about Christopher . . . " he blurted out eventually.

"Christopher? What about him?" Pastor Meyer demanded.

"He didn't do it," he continued in a rush. "He didn't . . . steal the Hampshire diamonds."

"We know he didn't, but how do you know?" Jill probed gently.

"What are you trying to tell us? Why have you come?" Pastor Meyer pressed insistently.

"Mr. Raynor said you wanted to see me about some information I passed on to . . . You won't tell the police, will you?" There was panic in his voice.

"I think I've been a minister long enough to recognise a guilty conscience when I see one," the pastor replied, amazed at the revelation so unexpectedly opening up to him. "What I said to Mr. Raynor was that I'd value a word with you concerning a man you met one lunch time in Byron's Bar. But I suggest you've now said too much not to say it all."

The pathetic youth appeared terror stricken and ready to seek escape. Then he sank down resignedly, his elbows on the table and his head in his hands.

"You won't tell on me?"

"I'm sorry, you must see how impossible a promise that is for me to make," Pastor Meyer objected. "If it is morally possible I'll keep your counsel, but I can't judge that until I've heard what you are going to say."

Lester jerked his head up. "I can't tell you who *did* steal the diamonds, if that is what you are thinking."

"What can you tell us then?"

"Not much, really." He took a gulp from his mug. "I don't know how you knew about my meeting with that chap in the cafe, but I almost wish I'd never met him, except that I was glad of the money."

"That wasn't the first time you'd met him?"

"The first time was in Raynor's. This dark fellow came in and started looking around the shop. Because of the way he was poking around, I went over and asked if I could be of assistance. He jumped, for he hadn't seen my approach. 'I'm not sure these are genuine sapphires', he told me, putting down what he'd been examining. 'In fact, I suggest you have quite a bit of junk in here.' I was as mad as anything and assured him that the sapphires were genuine in as offhand a manner as I dared. Carrying on as if everything was rubbish!"

He pushed away his mug, and Jill removed it to the sink. "I really was annoyed and informed him that we have some very influential customers, including Sir John Bentley Hampshire. 'Oh, I suppose you know him personally?' he said sarcastically, so I said I knew him very well — though I don't, really. He raised his eyebrows in a very mocking fashion and said he supposed I even knew where his safe was. I was so mad I answered before I thought what I was saying. 'Of course I do, and I'll tell you for a hundred pounds.' To my amazement, he took me up on it. Fair enough, I thought, for I was in a tight spot through betting."

"You must have realised by then what kind of man he was."

"Sure, but I thought he'd be unlikely to get away with anything. Anyway, I've no particular love for Sir John, for he's snubbed me often enough in the shop. So why should I care if he got robbed?"

"Did you know where his safe was?"

"Not until I'd found out from Christopher in a very roundabout way — he had been to Broad Acres several times. He'd no idea he'd told me anything significant."

"So you met the man to give him your information, then again when he paid you, the occasion that was witnessed. Do you know who this man is?"

"No idea — honestly."

"Anything else?"

"Isn't that enough?" He looked at the pastor

237

fearfully. "What are you going to do?"

"I'll tell you what I'm going to do, young man, I'm going to speak to you very straight. I can't see that it actually benefits anyone to broadcast your story, but I suggest you should listen to your conscience and think on your ways. Betting, unpayable debts, fraudulent gains and deception are paths which lead to ruin. Be advised by me and stop playing with fire. Consider what happened as a timely warning. However, I can't see that your conscience can ever be easy until you have the courage to do what you know to be right about the things you've told us." Then Pastor Meyer preached a summary of his Sunday sermon to him, and his congregation had never been more obviously uncomfortable.

To Addison's relief, the discourse was rudely interrupted by the telephone. When Pastor Meyer returned to the kitchen, the lad had gone.

"Who was that?"

"That," he replied, "was Dr. Mason with news at last of our irresponsible family and David and Paul. They are stranded miles away from anywhere, it seems, after a wild goose chase of some kind. He said we needn't be anxious, he knew exactly where they were, and he was just setting off to pick them up after ringing the Ransoms as well. What a family! No wonder I'm going grey!"

Jill was getting a snack ready for the two of them when there was yet another interruption. It was the sergeant Martin Meyer had seen that morning.

"Sorry to come at such an inconvenient time," he apologised, glancing at the table. "But it won't take a minute. Is your daughter at home? I'd like her to confirm the identity of the man on this photograph as the Tony Masterson they met last week." He showed them the picture of a distinguished, grey headed man.

Pastor Meyer apologised for his daughter's absence and explained all that they knew.

"They are very foolish," the sergeant told them. "It is no amateur gang they are prying into and they could find themselves in big trouble."

"They are safe enough, by the sound of it," the pastor assured him. "It's just a case of Dr. Mason picking them up. He didn't say where they are, exactly, but he knows the place."

"Dr. Mason? Did you say Dr. Mason — from Fair Haven?" the officer asked in sudden agitation. When both Martin and Jill nodded, puzzled by his attitude, he became at once crisp and business-like. "Do you mind if I use your phone?" he inquired rapidly. "I'm sorry, but I'm afraid those youngsters of yours *have* succeeded in walking into trouble. We already have our eyes on Dr. Mason regarding the Newton Gallery burglary and we are sure he is connected in some way with other offences. We do know for certain that he is no doctor. Neither is his real name Mason. Thanks." He hurried through to the study at Martin's invitation. "There is no time to lose."

Chapter 18

As Liz stood in her unsavoury hiding place, one emotion followed closely upon another. Fear took hold first on the realisation that she was alone with this man, a man with a gun within reach. Then anger superceded fear, giving her a desire to scream at him and fight him with her fists, but stubborn determination took over in time to prevent such a hopeless confrontation. And the more the minutes became hours, the greater became her determination and the more possible it began to seem that , far from all being lost, there was yet time for all to be won.

She dare not move in case the man was looking in her direction, so she just stood listening to his movements and under the breath mutterings until he finally walked across the room and turned off the light. Even then she dare not do anything for a considerable time, uncertain whether he were awake or asleep. In the meantime, she sought to fortify her spirits by silently reciting hymns of promise and comfort to herself.

> Leave God to order all thy ways
> And hope in Him whate'er betide,
> Thou'lt find Him in the evil days
> Thy all sufficient strength and guide.
> . . . God never yet forsook at need
> The soul that trusted Him indeed.

That was the kind of encouragement she needed. Her situation did not seem as bad when she saw it in the right perspective.

> God moves in a mysterious way
> His wonders to perform,
> He plants His footsteps in the sea
> And rides upon the storm.
> Ye fearful saints, fresh courage take,
> The clouds ye so much dread
> Are big with mercy, and shall break
> In blessing on your head.

'He plants His footsteps in the sea . . . ' Who can trace footsteps in the sea? So why should she fret because she could not yet see any evidence of God's positive interest in their affairs?

With a start, Liz realized that the man was snoring. Now that she had to move, she would have given anything to stay where she was, unpleasant though it might be. But as it was a case of 'nothing venture, nothing win', she forced herself to emerge into the room. There was only one thing she had to do and that was to find and procure the key to the boys' prison, but she knew that was no mean task. She had not heard him drop it into a drawer or on to any hard surface. If he had put it into his jacket pocket she could perhaps retrieve it, but the prospects were not so good if he had it in his trouser pocket! She must not rush things in case she should stumble into something in the darkness. Feeling carefully with her hands, she took a cautious step forward. A floor board creaked but the snoring continued, so she moved forward again. She must be within touching distance of the desk with its awful content. Her arms groped around in mid air until they came in contact with the solid surface they sought. Nothing but greasy dust on top. The drawer was open a fraction and Liz, her chest pounding, pulled gently until the space was wide enough for her to get her hand inside. She dreaded her fingers coming in contact with the cold metal of the revolver, her over active imagination anticipating a deafening report upon impact. But nothing happened and nothing else was in the drawer. One thing was certain, she would never dare enlist the aid of the gun herself!

Liz tried to remember the room. As far as she could recall there was an open space between the desk and the chair where the man had no doubt made his bed. She crept forward, praying that he would not hear her thunderous heartbeats, heartbeats that almost stopped when she came lightly up against his shoulder. Her knees buckled under her and she crouched on the boards, the tips of her fingers spread apart to keep her balance while she waited in panic to see if he would rouse. The man stopped snoring, gave a groan and stirred, making his chair creak. In that moment Liz imagined discovery staring her in the face, but then the snores resumed and she almost sobbed with relief. She allowed a few more minutes for safety then groped for the chair legs and followed them upwards, slowly and deliberately. The back of the chair was uncovered, so the man must have kept his jacket on. She did not blame him, for she was cold, too, but it added to her problem, calling for extra care. Her temptation was to hurry in order to get away from this man, but she forced herself to slow down. It took quite a while to work round the bottom edge of his jacket to where his pockets were, but her light fingers suddenly found what they were searching for. The joy and surprise of feeling that unmistakable hard object brought on an uncontrollable bout of trembling, much to Liz's concern and annoyance, for she had to wait until the worst had passed to proceed any further. Then the man stirred again and dropped his arm so that it hung down beside the chair, brushing her hand on its way. Liz was glad of the pitch darkness. She was sure she would not have dared to do what she was doing had there been a full moon shining through the window. Her fingers found the inside of his pocket. She was so close that she could feel his exhaled breath as he snored on.

A hooter blared somewhere in the night. It was

muffled and distant, but its suddenness jolted Liz's taut nerves and she gave the sleeping figure a sharp thump. He gave a gasp but, to her amazement, continued to slumber.

Seconds later, the key in her hand, Liz crept away, glowing now with thankfulness and hope, certain that it had been worth the ordeal, terrifying and unforgettable though it had been.

Having no desire to return to her former hiding place, Liz slowly tiptoed out of the room. In the corridor, she debated what to do next. She would find out first if the outside door was locked. It was, so she groped her way back up the stairs and on the corridor until she almost walked into the door of the boys' prison. There was no sound from inside. Her fingers touched the keyhole. Slipping the key into it, she turned gently. Almost without sound, the key turned. She locked it again, pocketed the key and turned away. There was no point in trying to release them yet, for Dr. Mason had said they wouldn't come round for some hours. Better to wait a short while, giving them all chance to awaken. She seemed to remember another door near that of the boys' room. She would conceal herself behind that for a while. A few seconds' blind groping along the wall and her intentions were easily carried out.

The room she found herself in was extremely cold and the floor boards felt none too safe beneath her feet so that she dare not step far inside. Having no desire to fall through the floor, she seated herself behind the door, her back against the wall, and wondered what the darkness was hiding. She was sure she would never get warm again. What was the point of this whole ordeal, anyway? The others couldn't possibly still have that crucial document, so they had no significant evidence against anybody. No-one would believe their story, Liz thought dejectedly. Dr. Mason would deny everything. Tony Masterson would deny everything. But they themselves would be in terrible trouble. They had their parents to face, and the police who were no doubt seeking them by now. In her weariness and anxiety, it was all Liz could do not to give way to tears, the more so because of the knowledge that it was she who had dragged the others off on this vain chase. Like the disciples of old, her faith was failing. Rather than experiencing that 'grace to help in time of need', at the moment she was in danger of receiving that gentle rebuke, 'Wherefore didst thou doubt, oh ye of little faith?' But it wasn't God she was doubting, she argued with herself, but the wisdom of her own precipitate actions.

Suddenly, overcome by fatigue, her body relaxed and her thoughts ceased to trouble her any more. She was losing touch with the ordeal she was living, and the one desperate attempt she made to rouse herself from drowsiness failed completely and she slumped sideways, sleeping peacefully.

Daylight was advanced when she awoke again. She sprang to her feet in panic when she realised she had slept so long. Then she heard the footsteps which must have roused her. They were not coming towards her but gradually getting fainter, so she guessed that the man was going down the stairs to the main entrance. The light filtering through the dirty glass showed the room up enough for her to cross over to the window without difficulty and she peered cautiously out. It was the same man she had robbed of the key and he was walking swiftly away across the cobbled yard. At the gateway he disappeared behind the high wall without a backward glance.

It was time for Liz to get busy again. Not bothering with quietness or caution, she fled down the way the man had gone, saw that he had not locked the door after him and sped back up again. Her fingers trembled as she fumbled with the precious key in the lock of the boys' prison, but she had no difficulty in getting inside, to be greeted by open mouths and incredulous stares. But Liz's elation dropped at the sight of Tony Masterson sitting with the three boys. Sensing her dismay, the man got to his feet immediately and went over to her. He put his hands on her shoulders and she looked into the clear blue eyes in bewilderment.

"Trust me," he said quietly, and he reminded her of the man they had first met. "I'm Tony Masterson," He smiled a lopsided, quizzical smile. "There's a twin brother around who isn't Tony Masterson, and I believe you've run into him once or twice. Is there no-one else around?" he ended urgently.

Liz hesitantly smiled back. "There's only one

man on guard, and he's just gone out, so let us get out, too!''

"We saw him go," Alan said, lingering by the window as the others made a dash for the door.

"He'll have gone for our breakfast — if you can call a teacake without butter breakfast," Tony said, "and he's not usually away for long. We've no time to . . ."

"Too late!" Alan groaned. "He's back."

"Lock the door, Elizabeth — quickly," Tony Masterson ordered, "or he'll find out you are here and that we have the key. How did you get it?"

"Out of his pocket when he was asleep," Liz laughed as she locked the door from the inside. "He probably doesn't yet realise it has gone. What'll happen then, we'll have to wait and see."

They heard the heavy boots approaching, then a muttered exclamation of annoyance. Those inside the room smiled in spite of their disappointment at not getting away, imagining the man's bewilderment on finding an empty pocket. The momentary silence was broken by the sounds of departure, slow and uncertain. The group turned instinctively to Masterson for guidance, but he shook his head.

"Let's see what he will do," he said in a whisper. "He just might have a second key." He turned to Liz. "We don't want him to see you here, so I suggest you make use of Paul's 'bed' which is most in the shadow. Put this coat over you. If David sits at this side, you'll not be noticeable from the door."

"There isn't much time." Liz replied, a catch in

her voice, as she took up her position. "They are clearing out at lunch time."

"There are plenty of us," David said. "If there's only one guard, can't we just walk out?"

"He is armed."

Alan turned sharply from the window. "He's out there," he told them, "searching among the cobbles. He must imagine he dropped it when he went out before."

They all crowded round the window where they peered through the dirty panes. Liz made sure she was hidden by the others, and they watched the stooping figure slowly and methodically covering his tracks. It was a typical November morning, not raining any longer but with a patchy fog clinging near the ground.

As they watched, a bunch of youths suddenly entered the yard with a rough wooden cart. They stopped short when they saw the figure already there and he looked up, startled.

"Clear off!" His voice floated faintly to the group above.

The boys did not move but glanced at each other as if debating what to do.

"Clear off yourself," the biggest one replied eventually. "We've as much right here as you."

The man waved his arm angrily. "Clear off!" he repeated in harsher tones. "What do you want? This is private property."

The big boy thrust his shoulders back. "We know it is. It belongs to my dad. Who are you?"

The man was clearly taken aback, but he made a credible attempt at bluff. "Oh, he's your dad, is he?" he growled. "Then you dad knows all about me being here, don't he? Put me here to guard the place against intruders, didn't he, because he'd had break-ins? So what do you want?"

The little group shuffled uneasily, waiting for their leader to speak.

"We only want our bonfire wood and our guy, Mister. From the room at the bottom of the steps — and, what's more, Dad knows we've come for it."

The man hesitated, seeing which the lads who had clustered somewhat behind their spokesman stepped forward with new courage. Obviously deciding there to be no potential danger in co-operating with them, and for the sake of not arousing suspicion in their minds, their challenger motioned them to pass.

"Be quick," he barked. "Get what you've come for and be off! Only that one room, mind you. No wandering about. It's not safe." He watched them move forward, then thought it necessary to throw a further word after them. "Only one visit, mind. I don't want you around all morning. What's the good of your dad giving me a job to do and then letting every Tom, Dick and Harry come mooching about?"

They didn't listen for any more. The man turned doubtfully away with an irritated gesture, then dropped his head to continue his search.

Tony Masterson didn't listen for any more,

either. "Quick, Open the door!" he commanded. "I've had an idea. It might work." He paused. "But I have to ask one question first. Are you all quite sure of me and of my explanation to you?" They nodded as Liz unlocked the door. "Elizabeth?"

"Yes." She smiled up at him. "I think I always hoped there was some explanation — and not only for Christopher's sake."

"Thanks. Then here goes," the older man said, obviously moved. "There's just a chance one of us can get through," he continued rapidly, "and I must go as I haven't time to explain. I'll be back soon with help." With which words he slipped out of the door and ran along the corridor.

"What's his idea? How can he get out?"

"Here we are, still asking questions," David said, sitting down resignedly. "We've also had plenty of practice at sitting waiting, so what's another day or two?" he ended with his old sarcasm.

"David!" Liz exclaimed. She turned the key and went over to him. "Are you still not sure of him?"

"Sorry, Liz," and David smiled a rare bright smile. "I really will have to drop the sarcasm from now on. In actual fact, at this very moment I feel more sure about more things than I have for a long time! I'm sure of Tony Masterson, I'm sure that we'll be the better for this ordeal, I'm sure I'm delighted to see the pretty fairy who's come to rescue us, and I'm sure my sins are forgiven at last, little as I deserve it."

Any further speech was completely smothered by

250

the pretty fairy herself flinging herself on him and hugging him until he could scarcely breathe. Paul took one glance at the situation and joined Alan at the window in disgust. "When I get older, I shall steer clear of all women," he said with laughing blue eyes rolling upwards. "Our jailor still down there?"

As if he had heard, the man looked up with a scowl.

"Yes," Alan replied unnecessarily. "But not a sign of Tony Masterson. I don't see how he can get out with Smiler standing there."

They continued to watch, but the only persons they saw leaving the building were the boys with their strange load of branches and boards that had been stored in a dry place ready for the much anticipated burning ceremony. Six of them had come and six left, two bringing up the rear with the cart, struggling over the cobbles while the substantial guy wobbled about amidst its nest of old drawers and sticks.

"Thanks, Mister," the spokesman addressed the man again, "We've got 'em all."

They got no reply, so the rather comical procession struggled slowly out to the road and disappeared.

David, suddenly catching Paul's laughing eyes, remembered that he should be feeling embarrassed and gently disentangled himself. "Let's compare notes," he suggested. "While we are waiting, we might as well fill in the picture — but one of you two stay at the window."

Alan glanced admiringly at his sister. "You did a good job," he said. "Though it beats me how you arrived so miraculously on the scene just now. How did *you* get here from Crow End?"

So they talked, sharing experiences and forgetting their cold and hunger for a while. Both Alan and Paul kept watch, though Paul did more talking than watching. Their jailor soon abandoned his search and presumably returned to his 'bedroom' to ponder on his misfortunes.

"It seems we've had our breakfasts!" Paul lamented.

"You shouldn't complain," Liz replied. You've had a meal since I have. It's exactly a day since I ate."

Of Tony Masterson there was not a sign.

Chapter 19

As soon as the sweating, struggling lads with the cart had toiled into the road and round the bend, the inanimate guy suddenly ceased to loll about and came to life. Bounding out of his conveyance, he halted his two carriers and the whole procession stopped, joining him in hearty laughter.

"Thank you, boys," Tony Masterson said, still smiling as he pulled off the woollen stocking and old hat from his head. "I wish I could tell you what this is all about, but I musn't linger. Perhaps you will see it in the papers, and then you'll know you had a hand in relieving a rather dramatic situation." He untied the string which had been tightly drawn round his ankles over the ragged and baggy trousers he was wearing to cover his own and removed the rest of his disguise. "But in the meantime, I did promise to make it worth your while, so perhaps you could make use of this between you."

The boys were so taken aback by the size of their reward that for a moment words eluded them. But not for long. With a solemnity fitting the occasion, the oldest boy received the money while they all stammered their thanks.

"Thanks, Mister," their treasurer said. "We were glad to help. Our club is saving up for a mini-bus so, if the others agree, I think we should put the money towards it."

Tony Masterson said goodbye to them and walked on, conscious that the little group was staring after him, full of questioning amazement.

"I hope they hear the whole story," he thought. "Most likely the money will end up in fireworks rather than in that mini-bus, but they were a bunch of good, sensible lads, all the same."

He looked around him. He was in a dismal area where all the adjoining streets looked alike, a monotonous sequence of dirty warehouses, tenement houses and scrap yards. He passed one seedy looking shop, and guessed that it was the source of his equally seedy diet during the days of his captivity. There was no-one about and no traffic on the road, and Tony wondered idly how the shop managed to pay. But it might be different during the week.

The scene changed so little that Tony began to wonder if he was going in the right direction. The boys had told him that the town centre lay in that direction, but they didn't know where the police station was. The other way, they said, led to the docks.

"As soon as I see anyone, I'll get proper directions" he told himself.

Presently, a car came cruising round the next bend. It's slow speed prompted Tony to put up a hand to make enquiries of the driver. Too late he recognised the man at the wheel. As Dr. Mason drew up alongside, boxes and suitcases surrounding him in the plush interior of his car, he looked as surprised to see Tony as Tony was dismayed to see him. Of all the unfortunate things to happen, this was surely the worst, and it was a situation which called for every bit of bluff Tony could muster. The outcome of this confrontation spelled either success or failure and he would not let those youngsters down again if he could help it.

"Hi, Boss!" The words seemed to be out even before he realised what he was going to say and in a flash he saw the line he must take. "All ready for off? Let's hope the sun's shining over the water."

Dr. Mason did not smile. "How do you come to be here so early, Nick? You're supposed to be bringing Joe at lunch time. What's happened."

Tony, knowing his brother's capacity for never being intimidated, waved an airy hand. "Don't worry, Boss," he said carelessly. "Everything's arranged. Joe'll be here when he said. Somebody brought me up a bit earlier. Never liked to be at the last minute."

Dr. Mason continued to frown. "Freddie O.K.?"

Tony, careful not to betray his uncertainty, presumed that Freddie was the man on guard in the warehouse and replied with brazen ease, "Sure, oh sure."

"And the kids?"

Tony laughed. "Suffering a bit of a hangover this morning, I believe. Nothing they won't soon get over."

"And where are you going?"

"Thought I'd just go along to the police station to let them know there are squatters in a building on there." He laughed again loudly. "Actually, I've just one thing to sort out before leaving this depressing place. Won't be long, Boss. See you later," and he jauntily resumed his walk towards the town.

He began to sweat now. The words had been given him. They were all true. But the underlying strain had caught up with him and he willed the doctor to move on, at the same time forcing himself not to look nervously round.

Dr. Mason was obviously a little uncertain and, in order to play safe, Tony abruptly turned off the street at a tangent and followed his former direction by a more devious route. He came to a row of black walled, identical houses. A group of people standing outside looked at him curiously when he inquired for the police station, but gave him the information readily enough.

"You'll find this street leads into a major road. Turn right and continue until you reach the traffic lights, where you turn left. You can't miss the police station, for it's a big, modern building only a few yards after the junction.''

The instructions proved correct and ten minutes later Tony walked through swing doors into the warmth and reassuring security of the police station. An inspector looked up as he entered and the constable leaning over his desk straightened his back and said good morning.

"Good Morning," Tony replied. "I've a job for you. Excuse the dramatics, but I have to inform you that several young people are being held prisoner in one of the disused warehouses in the docks area . . .''.

The inspector was on his feet. "Not the Meyer kids?''

"The same. You know about them?''

"There will hardly be a station in the country that doesn't know about them! Can you take us there?''

"That's why I am here — and to make a statement regarding the involvement of Christopher Meyer in the Hampshire diamonds case.''

"Am I speaking to Tony Masterson?''

"At your service — also having been detained for a considerable time against my will by those who sought to keep me silent.''

The inspector raised a restraining hand and gave orders to the constable. He then took up the telephone, spent several minutes talking at top speed to several other police departments then, taking Tony quickly by the arm, led the way outside.

What had seemed a considerable distance to Tony on foot, was covered by a convoy of three police cars in what seemed more like seconds than minutes, and Tony had no difficulty in locating the exact warehouse. Any doubts he might have had were dispelled by the sight of Dr. Mason's car standing on the cobbles.

"The owner of that car is the man you want," he told the inspector. "He's the brains behind this gang."

The actual capture of the crooks was an anticlimax after the dramatic nature of the previous events, for the element of surprise had caught Dr. Mason and his confederate completely off guard. The temporary unease at meeting 'Nick' Masterson on the road had not seriously affected Dr. Mason's complacency. Nothing could stop them now from getting away in time. One second he was virtually out of the country, the next he was handcuffed to a very business-like policeman. Typically, there was no rancour in his last remark to Tony Masterson as he was hustled into the police car. There were blurred faces at the window above.

"So the best men win. I congratulate you." He shrugged. "What a degrading end to a successful career — beaten by a handful of teenagers and a cat! Be sure to commend Paul in particular on my behalf. You could do worse than sign him up, Inspector."

The inspector smiled, in spite of himself, but continued impersonally and efficiently to supervise affairs.

Accompanied by a sergeant and Tony Masterson he went up to collect the waiting prisoners.

Somehow, no-one seemed inclined to speak. The sight of Dr. Mason being led away filled them all with mingled relief and regret, relief on Christopher's behalf, and regret in that they still found difficulty in regarding Dr. Mason as an enemy and a common thief. It was impossible to discard completely their old image of him, that of benevolent, teasing friend. So the party trooped silently down the stairs feeling none of the elation they would have expected from this moment. But it was what they had been working and waiting for.

Paul stopped suddenly, causing the others behind to cannon into him. There was consternation on his face as his hands went quickly from pocket to pocket. Turning, he attempted to push past David back up the steps but his brother held him and the rest stopped in their tracks.

"Let me go," Paul cried, struggling. "I've dropped my comic. It must have come out of my pocket in that room. It won't take me a minute to get it."

"Don't be childish," David retorted. "What's a comic? We can't hold the police up for that!"

"I want it," his brother replied defiantly, "or there'll be a gap in my collection."

"Go on, laddie. We'll wait for you," the inspector laughed. "I've got a boy of my own who would just be the same," and he winked a reply to Paul's grateful glance as he sped away.

Back in the station, they were given hot drinks and food, and their bodies began to thaw in the warmth of the room. David, at Liz's side, was concerned lest her physical condition should suffer after the way she had treated herself the last twenty four hours, but the sparkle was returning to her eyes and a smile to her lips in spite of her bodily fatigue. Alan and Paul, confident that the coffee was less potent than Dr. Mason's brew, drank cup after cup, declaring that they felt like taking a bath in it, too.

They were all happy to let Tony Masterson do most of the talking, content simply to add bits here and there when he was unclear of some detail and enlisted their help.

The inspector could see that they were all extremely tired, but he nevertheless had many questions to ask them, one of which concerned the fateful letter Dr. Mason had written to Joe.

"When you had the letter in your possession at Crow End, did you read any of the contents at all?"

"There was no time to read anything," David replied, "for we were interrupted almost immediately. Paul heard someone coming as soon as he picked it up, so he shoved it hurriedly behind the picture. I'm sorry we couldn't hang on to that letter, for it would no doubt have been of help to you, judging by the reaction of that lot to its loss."

"There's no need to reproach yourselves on that score," the inspector replied. "No doubt it would have told us a few things we don't know, but it would have been the height of folly to have tried Dr. Mason's patience too far. It's not too comfortable with a gun at your back is it, Paul?"

Paul got to his feet, his face flushed and trembling slightly. "I guess this has to be my moment of glory," he stated dramatically, but the moment was marred slightly by the unusual nervous squeak in his voice. "I don't suppose it will ever come my way again, so I might as well make the best of it."

Wonderingly, they all watched as slowly out of Paul's pocket came the comic and his mother's unposted letter. At least, out came the envelope his mother had addressed. But the blue sheet Paul drew out of that envelope was not written in his mother's hand at all.

"It was Mum's letter they burned," he told them. "I swapped them over in their envelopes when they were searching you, David. I could see you thought me demented when I started acting on, but it was all I could think of doing. As you know, it worked, for he separated us by taking you into the next room, but I admit I could hardly believe I'd got my chance!"

"You mean . . . you mean," David stammered, "that when Dr. Mason had hold of that . . . that envelope, he had actually got hold of what he wanted, without knowing it?"

"And gave it back to me," Paul laughed. "He would kick himself if he knew, don't you think? You've no idea how I was shaking inside, but I daren't let him see it."

The inspector took the sheet with a smile and the others, speechless, regarded Paul with a new respect. However, they must not let him see how impressed they were, or he would be too cocky for words afterwards!

The telephone rang and the inspector answered it, his eyes still on the document in front of him. Then he replaced the receiver.

"That was your parents, David," he told them. "They will be here in about half an hour. Your father says he is personally going to make sure you all get home, this time!" He smiled then tapped the paper with a pencil. "There is actually little here we did not suspect, but it gives us the proof we needed in a couple of cases. We are indebted to you, young man and to all of you for your contributions. However, take my advice and don't make a habit of meddling in such matters, for the outcome might not be as happy another time."

David, feeling like a reprimanded child, felt his indignation rising, then caught Tony Masterson's eye and returned his smile. After all, what had they to complain about? The ordeal, terrifying as it had been, was behind them now, and the experience had been all for gain, not only for Christopher but particularly for David, too.

"It will feel good to be home," Alan said longingly glancing at the clock.

"Your young lady is going to fall off the chair if she goes to sleep there," the inspector observed to

David, who blushed and gave Liz a little nudge.

Liz, quite unabashed, roused herself to speech. "I'm not really his young lady, Inspector," she said sweetly, "but I'd like to make an announcement right now for all the world to hear, that, whoever one day asks me to be his 'young lady' needs to know that in one respect I am different from most other girls. I think sapphires are the colour for me. Diamonds are definitely not my best friend — I never want to see another as long as I live!"